"I can't believe a state as progressive as Colorado would hang a human being just for stealing a horse!" Paula cut in.

Longarm explained, "Men are not hanged in Colorado for stealing horses, Miss Atwell. They are hanged so that horses are seldom stolen in Colorado. Stealing a man's horse in some parts of Colorado can be the death of a man with a blue norther or a locust plague headed his way and no horse to outrun either with."

He could see they were both eastern gals.

He said, "Laws out our way are different because *life* out our way can get different."

Paula asked, "Do you think that dumpy old man and those two young boys stole all those horses?"

Longarm shook his head and replied, "I suspect he's no more than what crooks call a *fence,* or a dealer in stolen goods. But when you catch a man with stolen army horses you can charge him with stealing them if you have a mind to. I mean to point that out to him, about this time tomorrow, after he's paced ruts in the cement floor by noon. They always expect a lawman to offer a deal in the morning. I'm sure a gent in his line of work has seen more than one horse thief hang . . ."

— TABOR EVANS —

LONGARM

AND THE HORSES OF A DIFFERENT COLOR

J

JOVE BOOKS, NEW YORK

THE BERKLEY PUBLISHING GROUP
Published by the Penguin Group
Penguin Group (USA) Inc.
375 Hudson Street, New York, New York 10014, USA
Penguin Group (Canada), 90 Eglinton Avenue East, Suite 700, Toronto, Ontario M4P 2Y3, Canada
(a division of Pearson Penguin Canada Inc.)
Penguin Books Ltd., 80 Strand, London WC2R 0RL, England
Penguin Group Ireland, 25 St. Stephen's Green, Dublin 2, Ireland (a division of Penguin Books Ltd.)
Penguin Group (Australia), 250 Camberwell Road, Camberwell, Victoria 3124, Australia
(a division of Pearson Australia Group Pty. Ltd.)
Penguin Books India Pvt. Ltd., 11 Community Centre, Panchsheel Park, New Delhi—110 017, India
Penguin Group (NZ), Cnr. Airborne and Rosedale Roads, Albany, Auckland 1310, New Zealand
(a division of Pearson New Zealand Ltd.)
Penguin Books (South Africa) (Pty.) Ltd., 24 Sturdee Avenue, Rosebank, Johannesburg 2196,
South Africa

Penguin Books Ltd., Registered Offices: 80 Strand, London WC2R 0RL, England

This is a work of fiction. Names, characters, places, and incidents either are the product of the author's imagination or are used fictitiously, and any resemblance to actual persons, living or dead, business establishments, events, or locales is entirely coincidental.

LONGARM AND THE HORSES OF A DIFFERENT COLOR

A Jove Book / published by arrangement with the author

PRINTING HISTORY
Jove edition / December 2005

Copyright © 2005 by The Berkley Publishing Group

ISBN: 0-515-14043-0

JOVE®
Jove Books are published by The Berkley Publishing Group,
a division of Penguin Group (USA) Inc.,
375 Hudson Street, New York, New York 10014.
JOVE is a registered trademark of Penguin Group (USA) Inc.
The "J" design is a trademark belonging to Penguin Group (USA) Inc.

PRINTED IN THE UNITED STATES OF AMERICA

10 9 8 7 6 5 4 3 2 1

Chapter 1

They held the Denver Stock Show after the fall roundup, when the thin dry air of the mile high city was cool and perfumed with the odor of burning leaves. Livestock competing for the blue ribbons had nowhere to go but where it was pent and if lots of folk could abide warm cow pats, horse apples were less aromatic and the jury was still out as to whether pig or chicken shit was most likely to make ladies of delicate feelings faint.

Hence, partly due to the cool weather but mostly because he was on serious government beeswax, Deputy U.S. Marshal Custis Long was wending his way through the maze of exhibits in the tobacco tweed outfit he'd been wearing on duty in town since President Rutherford B. Hayes and his handsome but fussy Lemonade Lucy had replaced the more casual and less honest Grant Administration.

In accordance with current Federal Civil Service Dress Code, Longarm, as he was better known to friend and foe alike, wore his three piece suit over a hickory work shirt and low heeled army boots he could walk or run in. He toted his double-action .44-40 cross-draw with its grips peeking out from under the tail of his coat.

The grips were utilitarian hardwood. But tailored to fit

1

his rawboned gun hand. And his six-gun was backed by a double derringer he tended to hold, like the badge pinned to his wallet, in reserve.

His black-coffee telescoped Stetson rode four-square cavalry style to shade his gunmuzzle gray eyes from a sun hanging white hot in a cloudless cobalt sky, despite the calender date.

Beside him, trying to stay in step on stubbier legs, strode Sergeant Nolan of the Denver P.D. in the blue uniform of the same, his badge now gilt instead of copper to a good extent because of the time a mere roundsman new to his job hadn't argued when a total stranger in Tobacco Tweed had flashed a silver badge his way and called, "I need a hand, here, pard!"

The resulting exitement had made the front pages of the *Denver Post* and *Rocky Mountain News* and, better yet, the modest federal deputy had passed on most of the credit to the Denver P.D. Allowing it had been Roundsman Nolan who'd first noticed those self-described moving men were putting expensive household furnishings from Paris, France, in that moving dray out back with nary a sign of the formidable Augusta Tabor, the wife of old Silver Dollar Tabor, supervising the proceedings.

The firm but fair society dowager had been a good sport about remarks to the effect she didn't allow her maids to dust such fancy stuff without her personal supervision, and her Silver Dollar, distracted as he might have been with that married blonde they called Baby Doe, had felt obliged to put in a word for Roundsman Nolan in high places.

Hence, when his old pal, Longarm, had asked Nolan's precinct captain for the loan of his old pal and a squad in blue to back their play, Nolan had told his buckos to listen sharp and do just as the damned Protestant might ask, adding, "Sure, Long might be a Saxon surname but this one is an American, now, like us, and there has to be a leprechaun or a changeling somewhere on his family tree, for

2

it's out of thin air the man can produce a double derringer and fire it like a Gatling gun!"

This was only partly true. Longarm seldom saw fit to show his badge or the bitty backup at one end of his watch chain and when he did, it only fired twice. But that usually gave him time to draw his more serious six-gun and those fool reporters were so inclined to magnify a saloon fight into another Northfield Raid.

Longarm wasn't expecting gunplay that afternoon at the fairground by the rail yards. A savvy lawman tried to cut down on the gunplay by having the other side boxed in, and knowing they were boxed in, before he said a word about anybody being under arrest.

And so Sergeant Nolan already knew where all the other buckos in blue were posted as he and Longarm approached the display of handsome saddle stock entered by a livery new to Denver and not yet on anyone's yellow sheets. They called themselves the Elegant Equestrian Establishment or Triple E brand and on this occasion, had entered show horses in the blue ribbon contest for the same, displayed when not competing, with livery mates for sale by appointment. No livestock was sold outright at the Denver Stock Show, lest it turn into a bustling market day, but nobody there raised stock just to brag on. Anybody who admired anything from a prize leghorn layer to a two-ton beef steer could ask for a business card with a view to doing business, later.

The handsome, freshly curried, mostly bay mounts, with a quartet of spirited gray geldings mixed in, had attracted a considerable crowd of folk who admired fine horesflesh.

Playing for time to size things up before he tipped his mitt, Longarm found a rail to prop an elbow over, near the gate. He had no call to tell the uniformed lawman with him what they were doing and where in the U.S. Constitution did it say a uniformed police sergeant had no right to lean on a rail and admire pretty horses?

3

It wasn't too clear what the pretty young things by the gate admired most. They didn't seem to know beans about horses. When the darker one told a fairer companion she just loved thoroughbreds, Longarm ticked his hat brim to them both and quietly observed, *"Standardbreds*, ma'am. They do look a heap like the breed of which you spoke, but they ain't. To be a thoroughbred a mount has to have papers tracing its thorough breeding back to exactly three Arab stallions brought to England before the American Revolution and bred to bigger but swifter than average English mares."

The fairer gal sniffed and allowed she didn't discuss such matters with gentlemen until after she'd been *introduced* to them.

But the brunette, a tad plainer of face with a nicer bottom, smiled at Longarm as she observed to her chum they'd *come* to the stock show to learn more about stock.

So when she asked Longarm to expain more, Sergeant Nolan tried not to laugh. Longarm gravely replied, "As one might well guess, ma'am, the price of an English thoroughbred with papers might well be spent on a yacht. That's how come they call them formal English horse races the Sport of Kings. But of course it's always been possible to breed mounts to the *standards* or overall appearance of a fancy thoroughbred, just by breeding less exhalted stock with thoroubred lines."

He saw the dismissive look cross her almost pretty face and quickly added, "That's not saying a handsome critter who looks like a thoroughbred can't have some thoroughbred bloodlines, ma'am. Those fancy lords in the old country refused to register foals whose sire or dam might not have a coat of arms on both sides and then, of course, they started out with Anglo-Arabic stock that was only human. When you get right down to it, a big brown horse with handsome lines is no more than a big brown horse with *racing* lines."

4

She said, "Oh, I see why these . . . standardbreds look like thoroughbreds, then. But how might a poor foal end up with one aristocratic parent and the other so . . . Never mind. I don't know you well enough to discuss such matters."

Longarm introduced himself and Sergeant Nolan. The brunette identified herself as Alicia Foxworth and said her chum was Paula Atwell. She added her pals called her Al. From the way the other one scowled, Longarm felt no call to assume anyone called her anything but Miss Atwell.

But as if to be a good sport, Paula Atwell observed those standardbreds didn't look much like the prize cowponies down the way and asked if it wasn't true cowponies had been bred from Arab stock as well.

Longarm nodded and explained, "Cowpony is a job description, not a breed, Miss Atwell. The usually cream Arabian and usually chestnut Berber mounts brought to Spain by the moors were smaller than thoroughbreds but bigger than cowponies. In both cases they were bred to other stock in an effort to wind up what was needed for the job. Speed and the ability to cover ground in the case of the thoroughbred, or standardbred, with the ability to zig and zag at a dead run in the case of the cowpony."

Interested in spite of herself, or mayhaps warming some to a strange man who was, after all, a lawman, Paula Atwell said, "At other exhibits down the line you see those cuter cowponies described as cutting horses, quarter horses, roping horses and so on. Are they different breeds or, as you suggested, job descriptions?"

Longarm said, "Both. It's natural to breed a critter good at its job to another of similar ambitions. But starting from scratch a *cutting* horse is a pony blessed with the ablity to read minds. It has to figure which of an assortment of cows its riders wants to cut out of the herd, Then it has to outthink any critter intent on heading anywhere else. A rider on a good cutter has it way easier than another riding a plain old pony."

5

The brunette who liked to be called Al said she'd heard a quarter horse was a cowpony who was one-quarter thoroughbred racehorse.

Longarm said, "I've heard that. I've explained how *costly* that might be. Others have said a quarter horse is a cowpony fast enough to enter in the quarter-mile races held in cow country, Miss Al. Thoroughbreds race up to four mile courses, albeit a mile and a quarter is the average. Few cowponies could run that far, fast enough to matter. But for that first quarter-mile they can streak as fast or faster on their shorter legs as any paid-up racehorse. So to keep such races exciting they're only a quarter-mile from start to finish, see?"

She said, "I do now, and it's obvious what a roping horse allows its rider to do."

It actually wasn't. But Longarm had been looking over the scene of a pending arrest for a spell and he doubted she really needed to know how a good roper knew when to slide to a stop and dig in its hooves against the snap of all that beef hitting the end of a tied-down throw-rope. So he just nodded.

He was saved having to explain why the U.S. Cav bought standardbred stock for its enlisted troopers when the jovial-looking cuss in charge of the display came over to join them, introducing himself as the one and original Jefferson Boyd of the Triple E and noting he'd noted they seemed interested in his horseflesh.

Longarm replied in an easy tone, "We were talking about those grays toward the rear. They seem to hang together, as if they came in a set."

The horse trader nodded and told Longarm he had a good eye, explaining, "The six of them carried members of the same army band. It's traditional for army bands and field grade officers to ride gray horses, with some of them favoring white. Got them six off the Army Remount Service as over-age-in-grade. Doubt even one of 'em could be older than eight or nine years. But you know those picky remount officers."

When Longarm didn't answer, taking time to choose his words so'd they'd stand up in court, the older man, Lord love him, asked, "Might you be in the market for such showy horseflesh, Mister . . . ?"

"Call me Custis," Longarm easily replied, adding, "Heard tell I ain't allowed to buy stock out here, during the show, but if I could have a closer look at those grays . . ."

"Come right in and look away!" said the horse trader expansively as he opened the gate. Sergeant Nolan stayed put and as the gate was closed again he quietly moved the two young gals back, saying, "Don't be after saying anything, ladies, but Longarm may be about to make an arrest and it's out of the line of fire he'd want you!"

"He's *Longarm*! The one we keep reading about in the papers!" gasped the hitherto reserved Paula Atwell. Her pal, Al, asked who Longarm was going to arrest.

Nolan confided, "Sure, some valuable army show horses were after being stolen south of town, at Camp Weld. It's fancy gray standardbreds they were and, sure, Longarm is about to be after asking them if they could be the ones!"

Paula sniffed, "That's silly. Horses can't really talk. Black Beauty is a children's fairy tale!"

The farm-bred Irishman replied, "I'm not one to be after reading English fairy tales, but a horse can tell you how old he may be, without saying a word, with his smiling *teeth*!"

Al asked, "Is that why you're not supposed to look a gift horse in the mouth?"

Nolan said, "It is indeed. An ever-shrinking sort of tree ring in the cutting surface of a horse's teeth tells you to within a year how old a darling horse might be. So the Army Remount Service sells riding stock off, at bargain prices, when it's seven years old."

"How old is that for a horse?" asked Al.

Nolan thought and decided, "Let's say thirty, in human terms. Sure, with spirit enough for most riders, if not to be after charging through Indian camps. Galvayne's groove, which is after appearing near the gum line, is the first sign a horse is after getting *old* and with proper care a darling horse will trot with yez at twenty. But the Cavalry has what yez might be calling *athletic* horses in mind."

Across the enclosure, Longarm had by this time looked all six Army grays in the mouth and felt it safe to say, "Mr. Boyd, ain't a one of these brutes more than five years old and you say you bought 'em off Army Remount?"

The horse dealer said, "I did, and I can prove it, if you'd like me to produce government bills of sale!"

Longarm smiled thinly and said, "Aw, I'm sure you can. I know I could if I set my mind to it with pen and ink aboard purloined blank Remount Service forms. We are still stuck with the self-evident facts of nature. The Remount Service never sells off five-year-old stock even when we're not having Indian scares and this summer we've had several."

He glanced around before he added, "I see the two young hands you had here have already lit out. You may as well know I had Denver P.D. circle you before I moved in. So by now they know they're under arrest and I hope you know better than to get yourself killed in front of such a crowd."

The one and original Jefferson Boyd shrugged and said, "I'll come quiet as a churchmouse, Longarm."

Longarm smiled thinly and said, "Flattery will get you nowhere, I was pretty sure you were on to us when those kids lit out as we were jawing. But I digress. Let me turn you over to Sergeant Nolan, now."

As Longarm took him by one arm to herd him out the gate, Jesserson Boyd protested, "Hold on! What are you talking about? All six of those horses were stolen, if they

8

were ever stolen, from the *federal government*, God damn your eyes!"

"Don't cuss in front of ladies," Longarm sternly replied as Nolan moved to cuff the horse trader's hands behind him. But Boyd was cussing fit to bust as Nolan led him off through the jeering crowd.

Longarm, having turned jurisdiction over to the local law, had no call to tag along and both the gals they'd been jawing with were young and pretty, too, and doubtless had what they called ring dang doos.

It was Paula, the somewhat brighter as well as prettier one, who asked what they were missing. She asked, "If you just arrested that man, aren't you supposed to take him to jail?"

To which Longarm easily replied, "He was hoping I might. That's how come I never. You see, ladies, whilst those stolen horses might have been federal property, they were stolen in the state of Colorado."

When neither seemed to follow his drift, he said, "The most any federal judge is likely to give a horse thief is ten years. Under current Colorado Statute Law, stealing one horse is a hanging offense."

Chapter 2

Seeing others in the crowd were hanging about as if to listen in, Longarm steered the two gals across the way, where some Shetland ponies were looking adorable, to confide, "I'd be proud to escort you ladies to the ice cream stand nigh the entrance if I didn't have to keep an eye on those now-untended horses. I wouldn't want you to think I was cheap. It's just that I'm stuck here 'til our pal, Sergeant Nolan, can send somebody to carry them off to the city pound."

Al gasped, "Are they going to put those poor horses to sleep?"

Longarm chuckled and explained, "That only happens to unclaimed strays after a number of days, Miss Al. When nobody claims anything valuable as a hog and up, the city can generally auction 'em off alive. Those six Army grays will surely be headed back to Camp Weld, once the Army provost marshal and the Denver district attorney work out the ways they want to handle such evidence. It'll be up to the one and original Jefferson Boyd whether he wants to stand trial in a state or federal court."

Paula Atwell asked, "I got the impression you weren't giving him that choice. Why do they call you Longarm?"

Longarm said, "My surname's Long and they do seem to

send me out on longer missions than some. As to offering choices to dead ducks, it all depends on whether he wants to sing for his supper or not. We mean to let him sort of marinate overnight in the county jail, considering the error of his ways. Tomorrow afternoon I mean to drop by and ask him if he'd care to be charged federal, in exchange for information on a whole lot of horse thievery that's been going around."

Paula asked, "Do you think that dumpy old man and those two young boys stole all those horses?"

Longarm shook his head and replied, "I suspect he's no more than what crooks call a *fence*, or a dealer in stolen goods. But when you catch a man with stolen army horses you can charge him with stealing them if you have a mind to. I mean to point that out to him, about this time tomorrow, after he's paced ruts in the cement floor by noon. They always expect a lawman to offer a deal in the morning. I'm sure a gent in his line of work has seen more than one horse thief hang by this time, so . . ."

"I can't believe a state as progressive as Colorado would hang a human being just for stealing a horse!" Paula cut in.

Longarm explained, "Men are not hanged in Colorado for stealing horses, Miss Atwell. They are hanged so that horses are seldom stolen in Colorado. Stealing a man's horse in, say, Chicago town just leaves him chagrined with no horse to ride. Stealing a man's horse in some parts of Colorado can be the death of a man with a blue norther or a locust plague headed his way and no horse to outrun either with."

He could see they were both eastern gals.

He said, "Laws out our way are different because *life* out our way can get different. For example, it's a penal offense to shoot a porcupine in the state of Colorado. It'll cost you a year in prison, not because they think a porcupine has more call than say a rabbit to live, but because a lost human with a gun can shoot most any critter. Whilst a porcupine is about the only edible critter a lost human can kill with a stick."

The prettier and brighter but more petulant Paula Atwell

pouted, "I hope I never have to eat a porcupine and I wish you hadn't mentioned the ice cream stand near the entrance! For I'm feeling hungry and thirsty and it seems I've been standing on these tired . . . limbs forever. Offer him one of our cards, Al."

Alicia reached in her purse to produce what surely seemed a business card. As she handed it to Longarm Paula suggested, "You may or may not care to come calling, with or without ice cream, any time this evening before eight. We have supper at eight and don't care to come to the door once we've started."

Longarm put the card away with a noncommittal nod, allowing he hardly ever disturbed ladies having supper. He let them fade away in the crowd before he fished the card out. Lest they take him for an anxious moon calf with no lady friends in Denver.

That was when he saw he'd been right. They were new in town and they'd set up, or were fixing to set up, as dressmakers in the new subdivision way the hell out along the Colfax Street car line.

It seemed a far piece to travel, even by horse-drawn street car, to order himself a new dress, even though it had been the prettier one who'd extended the invite. Sort of.

Life was too short for a man to worry himself as to what a cat or a mood-shifting gal might be thinking as they regarded you in much the same manner.

It only felt like a million years. He'd only smoked down four three-for-a-nickel cheroots by the time some hands from the city pound came by to take all that horseflesh off his hands. That left him free. He knew better than to leave by way of the entrance that ice cream stand commanded. If he wasn't headed halfways out to Aurora that evening he had no further call to jaw with dressmaking gals out that way and as their shapely memories faded he felt ever more certain he'd be spending the evening somewheres else.

For a bird in the hand was worth two in the bush when

bird in the hand was one hell of a lay and a good cook as well, speaking of suppertime.

Supper being off a ways and being in no hurry to get back to the old federal building that late in the day, Longarm soothed his innards and whiled away some time at a chop suey joint on Larimer Street, where he accepted with good grace how a Daughter of Han who'd sworn she would love him forever had taken up with some other white man, willing to take her away from all that chop suey.

The Daughter of Han who'd replaced her was moonfaced, flat chested and convinced she was too beautiful by half. But he left her a generous tip to show her she hadn't drawn blood.

After whiling away more time *near* the federal building at the Parthenon Saloon, Longarm reported in to discover his boss had left for the day and hence was in no position to saddle him with any further chores.

Hiding his disappointment, Longarm took his time legging it up Capitol Hill to Sherman Street so he could report the arrest and his planned follow-up to his boss, Marshal Billy Vail. Old Billy hardly ever put him to yard work around his big old brownstone. As Longarm approached through the cottonwood shadows across sandstone walks and leaf-littered lawns in the soft light of gloaming he saw his somewhat older and way dumpier superior seated on his front steps in after-supper shirtsleeves, smoking one of those impressive, expensive and Gawd-awful black cigars he likely had smuggled in from the nether regions.

The balding Marshal Vail had one of those ruddy faces that reminded one of a chubby infant having teething problems, and getting mighty pissed off about 'em.

Lighting a way-cheaper but less lethal cheroot in self-defense, Longarm sat upwind of his boss to fill him in on the arrest and his plans for a follow-up the next day.

Vail heard him out, but groused, "I dunno, old son. We don't get old and wise on purpose. We get wiser, thinking

14

back as we get older, on all the things that could have gone wrong and did. I put our Henry to work on the files as soon as reports about those noticeable gray Army band mounts came buzzing in like flies around a horse turd. So I can tell you, this evening, Jefferson Boyd has been arrest four times and convicted once in a career spanning thirty odd years."

He blew an octopus cloud of pungent smoke, stared morosely in to it as if for inspiration and added, "The one time he was convicted he copped a plea to a lesser charge for time served. The son of a bitch in sum is smart. So how come he was showing them band mounts at the Denver Stock Show less than a week after they were reported missing just south of dammit Denver?"

Longarm said, "I'll ask him. The prisons of this land of opportunity are not, by definition, institutions of higher learning. If crooks never made mistakes we'd be in a hell of a fix."

He stared thoughtfully through a tidier smoke ring and added, "What if the thieves who raided Camp Weld never told Boyd where they'd stolen them?"

Vail shrugged and muttered, "What if the dog had never stopped to shit and caught the rabbit? What's that old church hymn you're forever singing at times like these, old son?"

"Farther Along?"

Vail said, "Yeah, that, too. Farther along we'll see what we're missing this evening. Until then, we just have to hang tough, I reckon."

Longarm agreed. Vail asked if he'd care to come in for some coffee and when Longarm allowed he had other fish to fry the older man sighed and told him, "I hope you and that widow woman know all the other ladies along Sherman think the two of you are having too much fun by far!"

Longarm allowed he had no idea what the ladies might be gossiping about and they parted friendly, with Longarm humming at first and then softly singing to himself in the gloaming . . .

Farther along we'll know more about it
Farther along, we'll understand why
Cheer up, my brothers. Walk in the sunshine
We'll understand it, all by and by

He'd always wondered how words that sensible had been taken up by the Sunday school back home in West-By-God-Virginia. For they'd never inspired the sort of questions that could get a Sunday school kid stood in the corner, but laid things out as mere mortals could only hope to understand. He figured he'd understand what in thunder the one and original Jefferson Boyd was up to farther along. Nobody was fixing to tell him that evening.

And the evening was young.

The widow woman with the soft brown hair who lived a few crossings to the south along the same street had been left a heap of mining property in the Front Range by an older man Longarm felt sure had died with few if any complaints about the warm-natured woman he'd left behind. A feature Longarm found mighty attractive was her reluctance to have her name linked in the society columns with any mere mortal working for a salary. Hence their relationship had survived that stage where most gals expect a man to propose or get out of their way to the altar. She'd once confided during a naked pillow conversation that, were the truth to be known, few well-off widow women were looking to hitch up again in a world where any property a woman might own became her husband's in the eyes of the law. Any widow woman who could bear up under the strain had as much freedom to live her own life for her own pleasures as any man of the same wealth.

And so it was with a clear conscience Longarm cut east at the corner to slip along her back alley and enter by way of her kitchen door, as he was expected to at that hour, seeing as none of her neighbors would be out back hanging washing, whilst inclined to observe all that transpired out

16

front from many a bay window along Sherman Street.

But as many a man had learned before him, there were more ways to cross a woman socially than there were ways in that *Kama Sutra* to screw her, and so as luck would have it, that time, the widow with the light brown hair got pissed at him for barging in her back door, as she put it, whilst she had been in the act of paying her cleaning woman off and sending her home for the damned weekend.

There was nothing the three of them could say about it until after the cleaning woman left, not looking at him. Then the lady of the house lit in to him as an ill-mannered country bumpkin who knew less about conducting a "discreet assignation" as she put it, as he did about good breeding.

To which Longarm could only reply, not unkindly, "The last time I came to the front door you threw a hissy fit. As to my breeding, my poor but honest parents were married up in the eyes of their church well before my nativity and, seeing that ain't good enough for Sherman Street, we'll say no more about it and I'd best be on my way."

As he turned to march out the same door he'd come in by, the widow with the light brown hair gasped, "Custis! Where are you going? Come back here, you silly! Mamma forgives you!"

It would have been as bitchy to say he didn't forgive her. So he just kept going. She might have chased him across her backyard, but there was another day servant leaving next door, with that lady of the house seeing her off.

As Longarm and the servant gal reached the back alley about the same time, Longarm called loud enough for all to hear, "Allow me to escort you 'round to the streetlamps out front, miss. Seeing we seem to be headed the same way. I was just now delivering a package to the service entrance back yonder. My friends call me Custis."

The maid allowed she knew who he was and took his arm with a toss of her head as they vanished from view down the alley.

They parted friendly a few minutes later when she headed down the slope of Capitol Hill to where she dwelt west of Lincoln Street. He ambled on past the Vail house and beyond, across the statehouse grounds to Colfax Avenue.

There, he followed the brighter lights east as far as an ice cream parlor near the big Papist cathedral, where he picked up a gallon of marbleized chocolate and vanilla, hoping it would last 'til it could be delivered.

It did. Thanks to the crisp fall evening and the grade being flat for the draft horse pulling the streetcar, east of that awesome grade up from Broadway.

Longarm had once saved the very life, or so she'd said, of Miss Morgana Floyd, Head Matron of the Arvada Orphan Asylum, when another streetcar of that very line had run away with her and a whole raft of zoo-bound orphans. But Arvada, and Miss Morgna Floyd, were way the hell off to the west that evening and he'd already figured he'd never get to darken *her* door at a reasonable hour. A man had to think ahead before he got to darkening doors on gals.

When he got to the address suggested by the business card of Al and Pal, as he'd commenced to think of them, Longarm saw it was a private recently constructed cottage, albeit with a sign by the door allowing they made dresses inside.

The streetcar had clanged on and there was nobody in view as Longarm twisted the doorbell key. He figured this was just as well when Al, or Alicia Foxworth, came to the door in no more than her bare feet and a see-through shimmy shirt.

As she smiled radiantly up at him, Longarm gulped and said he hoped he hadn't arrived too late with his ice cream.

As she took the cardboard bucket from him Al demurely replied, "We've been expecting you since sundown. We were afraid you'd gotten cold feet. Step inside and let me shut this silly door. I'm afraid you'll find Paula is not quite as modestly dressed as me, right now."

Chapter 3

When Paula Atwell joined them in the kitchen Longarm figured it was safe to call her Pal. She'd literally let her fair hair down and that was all that was covering her perky tits, sort of. She had on a pair of French pantaloons but they were silk and thin enough to see she was fair haired all over.

She plopped her somewhat broader hips down at the kitchen table as if used to receiving company nigh naked. As Al dished out three bowls of ice cream and put what was left in their icebox it developed the two of them had been artist's models back east before they'd taken up dressmaking. They'd found fewer art classes to pose for in the less-refined west, they said. That was what they called country where folk kept more clothes on in mixed company, less-refined.

Longarm allowed he could abide refined manners, seeing he'd spent more time with some in Indian country. He warned himself, as he felt his way, how it was all too easy to take *different* standards of modesty for *no* standards of modesty. Those ancient Romans had traipsed around half bare-assed and they'd still slaughtered a slew of Etruscans after one of 'em had raped that Miss Lucrecia.

He knew many a white man had lost his scalp by mistaking the flash of bare Indian flesh for an invite. Unwelcome advances were as unwelcome to a stark-ass naked gal as they might be to one all gussied up in whalebone and chin to toe brocade. So he hung up his hat, shrugged off his coat and gunbelt when so invited, and sat down to eat his ice cream like a gent as he waited to be filled in on the rules of the house.

He could only hope it wasn't the sort of house as charged visitors who visited. He feared the social gaff he'd be making if he asked, and it wasn't. The trouble with those new "Bohemian" society rules made up by the toffs of Bloomsbury or artistic fops of Greenwhich Village was simply that social situations with no rules at all were harder to get going. For say what one liked about the often prissy rules of the late Victorians, at least they were *rules* one could break or follow as one chose. It saved a heap of hopping and skipping when it was understood up front that the gent walked a lady down either side of a street betwixt her skirts and the horse shit thrown up by passing traffic. In every town in the English-speaking world it was understood there were quality parts of town where everyone acted right and riff-raff parts of town where a person of quality ventured at their own peril. Longarm had recently been amused, but understood, a newspaper interview with a young lady of North-Field, Minnesota, who'd been a schoolgirl there the day the James and Younger boys shot their way out of town. But when they'd asked how she and her schoolmates had reacted to such famous gunplay she'd demurely replied they hadn't noticed it. She'd said, "Ruffians were forever firing guns over yonder, where they served hard liquor and worse. But none of us *proper* youth paid much attention to such goings-on."

Had Al and Pal been proper Victorians of any age there'd have been no doubt as to why they received gentlemen callers in their underwear. But he decided he'd pay out more rope and just eat his damned ice cream for now. He'd only later discover how *sophisticated* that had made him seem to their artistic eyes and verified all they'd heard about Denver's answer to Don Juan as well as Wild Bill, now that both those gentlemen were dead.

It was a tad late in the year for evening ice cream parties and if the more warmly dressed Longarm didn't notice, the bare breasted Pal pushed what was left of her own ice cream away, allowing she feared she might be coming down with a chill.

Al asked if it was too early to go to bed and added, "We'd all feel snugger under the covers."

Longarm didn't say anything. He wasn't sure what an artistic cuss ought to say. But when Pal allowed that seemed a sensible suggestion and Al took Longarm by the hand to lead him, he just grabbed his gunbelt in passing and went along to take his beating like a man.

It helped when neither gal suggested striking a light in the darker bedroom. It wasn't too clear which one was unbuttoning his shirt or which was working on his pants. But as he wound up across the covers kissing the prettier Pal that had to be Al offering an enthusiastic French lesson to his old organ grinder.

Not wanting to waste ammunition as he sensed he was in for a Battle Royal Longarm hauled Pal's French pantaloons down as Al did the same favor for him. Al was beating on his bare behind with her fists, complaining she'd gotten that erection up, gol durn it, as he rolled betwixt the welcoming thighs of Pal and shoved it where she demanded it. As he entered her Pal gasped, "Ohmigod! I'm already coming and it'll serve you right if I pass this baton to you in all its glory, Al!"

So the three of them were laughing when Longarm whipped it out of Pal just in time to come in Al as she gasped, "Sweet Jesus! You might have *warned* me!"

So a good time was had by all, if down and dirty barnyard rutting was one's notion of a good time. But as Longarm had noticed on other occasions he'd been offered a horny schoolboy's wet dream, the game of three in a tub was a tad overrated in real life.

As Longarm had always been too polite to say at such times, rutting with two gals at once allowed some mighty unusual positions and felt raw as hell besides, but after that it offered more to the sort of cuss who jerked off in the bunkhouse with a collection of French post cards than it offered a gent who really enjoyed making love to real women.

Good old country slap and tickle with a good old gal was one thing. Once the bed got more crowded things commenced to drift from country slap and tickle to freak show showing off and, if the truth be known, an oddly shy reluctance to let oneself go with either gal as one played musical pussy games. For those tender moments that punctuated a regular roll in the feathers with one gal felt too silly to indulge in before a third party, even one you'd just pulled out of with such feelings toward *her* held in lest they sound silly.

So Longarm wondered, as he tried to pleasure two gals at once, how one or more of them might be wishing at that very moment there were just the two of them in a less athletic position.

It was only after they'd all come in some unbelievable ways that the prettier-faced and more moody Pal, or Paula, commenced to cry and shove the shaplier and less-complicated Al's head out of her lap, protesting their male guest was likely to take them for a pair of perverts.

Al rolled over on her back, exclaiming, "Wheee! I don't care how I come or who I come with, as long as I get to come. And if that makes me some sort of pervert I say bring it on!"

Pal snuggled closer to Longarm, asking if he'd ever heard of an artistic sort called "Bisexual."

When he allowed he had, Pal said, "Lesbians are queer. Bisexuals are just *practique*, as the French put it."

Longarm chuckled and said, "The French are as good as the Greeks when it comes to having a name for most everything. I ain't sure I hold with such scientific titles. When folk get horny and desperate to come, they tend to come with anyone or anything on tap. Animal, vegetable or mineral, of either sex."

Al brightened and confessed, "I tried it with a dog, one time, but it didn't work. The fool pup kept pulling it out and licking it."

Pal gasped, "Al, that's disgusting!"

Al shrugged her bare shoulders and demurely replied, "You're one to talk, considering it was you who taught me to . . ."

"Don't you *dare* say it in front of a *man*!" Pal sobbed as she slapped at her fellow . . . dressmaker.

Wrapping a bare arm around either, Longarm soothed, "Lets keep this a friendly orgy, ladies. Ain't nothing either of you can confess that this dirty old cuss can't likely top."

As he'd hoped, that inspired both to ask what he'd ever done as vile as beastiality or queering another man. So in the interests of peace Longarm told them, perforce falling back on things he'd heard in barracks, bunkhouses and guardhouses, along with things he'd read in books compiled by doctors treating sex fiends and of course the forbidden books of Casanova, De Sade and such.

He wasn't certain he bought that yarn about a Paris house of ill repute where some of the whores were goats or pigs gussied up with silk ribbons and French perfumes, either, but he assured them soberly a goat in heat carried on more willingly than your average pig, while pigs were more willing than dogs, because that's what the books had said. When he got to where that Koran commanded Sons of the Prophet to never eat any goat they'd fucked, Pal insisted he was just making that up. But seeing he had her in a better mood with his own dirty stories, Longarm never insisted he'd never made that up.

Having heard him confess to perversions that were likely impossible, the naked ladies cuddled up to him felt more willing to discuss earlier adventures in that same bed, leading Longarm to wish he'd never gotten them started. For, again, the pool hall fancies of the pimple-faced had a tendency to strike grown men as trying-too-hard.

For as most men learned, growing up, it was dumb to make your fool self sick on Dad's cigars or put away Mom's apple pie until you puked. Grown men found those Roman gluttons who *made* themselves puke, so's they could eat still more, pathetic. A man trying to inspire yet another erection by molesting kids or the hired help was beneath contempt. Not just because he was acting dirty, but because he couldn't get it up without acting dirty.

The magic cure for impotence, as more than one sensible sawbones had tried in vain to assure a sex fiend, involved no more than leaving the fool thing alone until it was ready to go again. Nobody tried to revive his appetite after a full course meal unless he was a Roman glutton and a man in bed with a good-looking woman and a limp dick was most often a man wearing a satisfied smile, if he had a lick of sense.

So well before midnight, that night, Longarm felt certain he would never in this world get it up again and this didn't worry him because he knew from experience he would, after giving the poor thing some rest.

So he tried to change the subject to the coming dawn, wishing like hell it was later. He explained that much as he dreaded the thought he'd have to leave early, despite what he'd told that horse dealer, to work things out with both the Denver D.A. and the Remount officers from Camp Weld.

As he'd hoped, that inspired gals new in Denver to ask where Camp Weld might be. He told them it lay south of Denver on rolling prairie and explained the post was used by the Colorado Guard, the U.S. Cav and of course the Remount Service to break in new cavalry or artillery mounts.

Al, Lord love her, said she'd almost layed a dragoon, one time, and asked him what the difference betwixt a dragoon and a cavalryman might be.

He explained, "Not much, out our way. In theory a dragoon rides to the battle site and dismounts to fight on foot, whilst a cavalry trooper fights mostly on horseback. But in practice our Indian-fighting Army spend a heap of time tracking Mister Lo on foot."

"Mister Lo?" asked Pal.

"As in Lo, the poor Indian," Longarm explained. The jest had worn thin out their way, of late. He said, "The Mescalero played tag along the border with both the Mex and U.S. Cavalry all summer and they keep saying Sitting Bull is on his way back down from Canada. That's likely what's driven the price of American standardbred's so high. The Army is in the market for as many as they can come by. Heaps of other folk would rather set a standardbred than any of the more common breeds. In the morning, before I try to break Jefferson Boyd down, I want to make dead certain we have his head in the noose. A deposition from the Army to the effect those six gray band mounts were stolen from Camp Weld would be fun to wave in his fool face."

As he'd hoped, his digression had served to bore them as well as take their minds off slap and tickle. So the three of them wound up catching a few hours' sleep under the quilts, as snug as they'd promised, and in the morning, just as *he'd* promised, damned if he wasn't able to get it up again after all. So their three in a tub resumed and by the time he got out of there that morning, walking funny, Longarm was afraid he might have hurt himself.

Having been served a breakfast of ice cream and nymphomania, Longarm got off the streetcar when it got to Larimer for a more substantial meal of roast beef smothered in chili and topped with fried eggs, along with plenty of black coffee. He somehow wasn't in the mood for any chocolate covered donuts that morning.

Feeling more human, Longarm ambled on to the city pound, which was in point of fact a complex of pens large and small across the rail yards, by the South Platte, where the higher water table made for easy pumping. You pumped lots of water for critters ranging from stray dogs to wandered-off milch cows.

As he approached the corrals where they impounded horseflesh, Longarm saw he was running late. Denver lawmen and uniformed officers of the Army Remount Service and the Provost Marshal were already gathered there, to sort of hover like horse flies around the stock driven over from the Triple E display at the stock show to the north.

Longarm knew most of the old boys there, at least to nod to, and he'd elbowed up to the bar in the Camp Weld Officer's Club with the Remount vet from the same. Hence it was with a clear conscience and a cheery howdy he joined the bunch, asking, "How do you reckon we want to work things out for the prosecution, Doc? Your John Henry on a deposition ought to be way tidier to present in court than evidence as ain't housebroke."

The Army vet gave the floor to a major from the Provost Marshal's, who said, "We were just discussing that, Deputy Long. Some of it is and some of it isn't and if Jefferson Boyd dosen't beat the rap he has a nitwit for a lawyer!"

Logarm frowned and said, "Come on, gents, not a one of those so called over-age Army mounts was old enough to have been sold off by any Remount officer who wasn't blind!"

The military lawman replied, "No doubt of that. The doubt creeps in as one considers nobody has reported one of those grays we can't identify as having been *stolen*. A U.S. brand alone doth not a stolen anything make. Have you any idea how much surplus government stock is out there all around us? We can't even prove those grays were ever band mounts!"

A Denver lawman in plain clothes morosely came forward to observe, "We have no complain'tant missing half the stock and he only has to get one juror to believe he accepted a blizzard of bills of sale in good faith. So you can have him, we don't want him, he's too sure to walk for any DA in an election year!"

Above the growl of agreement Longarm pleaded, "Give me the seventy-two. We can hold him on suspicion and, meanwhile, let me see if I can get one of those horses of another color to talk!"

Chapter 4

It was a hell of a way to treat his store-bought tweeds, but they were due a dry cleaning, anyhow. So as everyone else lost interest and commenced to drift away, Longarm borrowed a rope halter from one of the hands at the pound and went for a ride along the river, bareback, on one of the grays in question.

The South Platte being mayhaps a furlong wide and inches deep as it wound through West Denver, at low water sand flats extended along its uncertain banks and the morning air was dry and crisp as well. So he heeled the gray forward and a healthy young gelding who'd been pent up in crisp weather should welcomed the chance for a frisky lope. The big gray didn't. It trotted mayhaps thirty paces and then, since the pesky stranger on its bare back wasn't wearing spurs or licking it with a quirt, it fell back into a willing enough walk.

Not having an Army band handy, but seeing nobody seemed near enough to laugh at him, Longarm threw back his head to sing in a not bad baritone.

Well, we belong to the Cavalry!
Now don't you think we oughter?

We're headed down to Richmond Town,
To give the reb no quarter!

It worked. The band mount pricked up it's musically trained ears to prance in time with the beat of the doggeral verse. But not with the enthusiasm a parade horse passing in review was supposed to show after plenty of rest on a crisp morning.

Swinging the gray around by the rope halter, Longarm told it, not unkindly, "You ain't used to the altitude out our way, I see. But don't you worry, pard. It generally takes a man, or a horse, about a week or so to get over Mountain Sickness. Your low altitude bone marrow churns out the extra red blood cells in no time."

He rode the gray back to the pound, asked them to see it got plenty of water and made his own way to the federal building closer to Broadway. It sure beat all how a man enveloped in tobacco smoke that smelled like burning garbage could smell another thing, but as Longarm entered his oak paneled office old Billy Vail looked up from behind his acres or so of cluttered desk to sniff and ask, "Where the hell have you just been, old son? Smells like you've been herding cows aboard a dying pony!"

Longarm nodded and said, "Close enough," as he sat down and lit up in self-defense before explaining he'd treated himself and a pent-up mount to a morning canter.

When he added, "Poor brute was heaving and sweating by the time I got him back to the pound," Vail nodded knowingly and rummaged through the papers on his desk.

Finding what he was looking for—nobody else could make sense of such a mess—the marshal said, "Here she is. These bills of sale just beat you here from the D.A. If I didn't drink with Governor Pitkin we'd be out of luck. They're still passing the son of a bitch back to us come Monday."

Waving the sheaf of government forms, Vail added, "Says here all four mysterious grays were sold off by Remount out of Fort Leavenworth."

Longarm protested, "That explains why the one I rode ran out of breath so sudden. But neither he nor any of the others was a day over five!"

Vail replied, "I noticed when I read the arrest report. Waiting on the answer to a wire Henry got off to Leavenworth on the Big Muddy this morning. We're talking about across the same from Missouri, and Missouri is the breeding center of mules and saddle horses."

He blew another octopus cloud and leaned back to pontificate on central locations and calcium-rich soil.

"I've heard tell of Missouri mules and bargain show horses." Longarm cut in, getting even by adding, "Cost you more for a thoroughbred raised on Kentucky blue grass or a Tennessee Walker. Best cowponies still hail from Texas, though."

Vail looked pained and replied, "Nobody's reported a rash of missing cowponies. Nobody rides the runty critters but cowboys and that's why they cost so little. Price of standardbred stock's gone through the roof with the War Department bidding for most anything that resembles one if it tops fifteen hands and ain't more than five or six. Don't you just hate it when the infernal Apache and Sioux get to war dancing at the same time?"

Longarm blew a thoughtful smoke ring and observed, "Ain't certain how I'd sell a horse I stole to the Remount Service, though. They can be so fussy about a pony's papers."

Vail nodded his bullet head to reply, "Damned A. But meanwhile heaps of Fancy Dans who like to ride proud but don't have the pocket jingle for the real thing pay as much as they can afford for a high-stepping if somewhat over-the-hill Cavalry mount. Old Army bays offer good value and a buyer lulled by that Army brand and a federal bill of sale ain't as likely to be suspicious as some. So the most serious problem a dealer in surplus Cavalry mounts might boil down to is a steady supply of surplus Cavalry mounts, with every Cavalry post in this land of opportunity well supplied with the same."

Before Longarm could answer, Old Henry, the young squirt who played the typewriter and kept the files out front came back with a Western Union telegram.

Henry had already opened it, of course, but he graciously allowed their mutual boss to read it and weep. "Leavenworth ain't missing any gray band mounts. Albeit they've bitched somebody sure ran off with a dozen bays a week ago Sunday. The interior guard they mean to court-martial says he never saw those ponies leave the post. It's hard to see such sights when you're up in the hayloft, fast asleep."

Longarm sighed and said, "I used to hate pulling interior guard on a weekend with nothing going on, knowing it was only when you deserted your post that anything was bound to happen. But if Leavenworth's been hit and Camp Weld's been hit . . ."

Vail assuered him, "We've sent out an all points to federal facilites west of the Cumberlands. Indian agencies and the postal service buying standardbred stock. Remember that Indian agent down to the Mescalero Reservation, shot by Billy the Kid during a raid on his agency's riding stock?"

Longarm nodded and said, "Joe Bernstein, a man with hair on his chest who deserves to be remembered more. Stood up to at least six or seven as they rid in to steal the agency remuda. He lost, of course, but that don't heap much glory on Billy the Kid."

Vail said, "Whatever. My point is that they were after agency stock because they could unload it for serious money. When you can buy yourself a good cowpony for less than a month's pay from an up-and-up dealer, the markdown for stolen goods gets ridiculous."

"What's the Remount Service bidding on a standard-bred as meets it's standards, this fall?" asked Longarm. Adding, "Last year prices on horseflesh ranged from two dollars a head for unbroke mustangs to four figures for a thoroughbred, with a good saddle mount with uncertain pedigree going for as much as two hundred."

Vail said, "Might get three hundred for a prime cavalry mount during an Indian scare. Seeing a sold-off vet goes for a quarter or less of what the taxpayer paid for it, we're still talking forty dollars or more."

Longarm objected, "But, seeing they ain't selling seriously *old* nags at old nag prices . . ."

Vail nodded and said, "It's up for grabs how many buyers think they're getting a bargain and how many know damned well those bills of sale don't mean toad squat. Either way, it's nigh impossible to get a conviction if the one found in possession has papers indicating he paid for it."

"Then the one and original Jefferson Boyd . . ." asked Longarm.

Vail shrugged and said, "Him, too, now that it's getting so uncertain how much stock in his possession was ever stolen."

Spying the look in Longarm's eye, Vail said, "Before you cloud up and rain all over me, there's no argument no Remount officer should have sold off those grays that neither Camp Weld nor Fort Leavenworth seem to be missing. But whilst we can hold a cuss under suspicion for seventy-two hours there's just no prison time mandated for suspicion alone. I agree it hardly seems fair. But there you are!"

Henry came back in, frowning thoughtfully. When Vail asked if Henry had any replies to his all points yet, Henry shook his head but said, "Missouri. All roads lead to Rome and eight out of ten Army mounts are born and bred in Missouri."

Vail cocked a brow at the sort of goofy-looking kid and expansively replied, "Why, thank you, Henry. I never might have guessed Missouri was stud farm country."

Longarm suggested, "What he might be getting at is Fort Leavenworth being where they sure foal big brown saddle mounts, is the headquarters for the Remount Service of the Army of the West."

Vail chuckled fondly and declared, "Wonders never cease around here. Everybody knows Army Remount buys, breaks and distributes cavalry stock out of Fort Leavenworth. What of it? Ain't we been getting beefs about purloined cavalry mounts from all over the damned west?"

Henry nodded but pointed out, "Offered for resale with bills of sale forged on printed U.S. Army forms, sir. It just occured to me what a bother it would be to steal blank forms every time one raided an Army corral. On the other hand, if someone started out with a whole bunch of forms lifted from the office supplies of a big headquarters post . . ."

"How do we go about proving that?" Vail cut in.

Longarm asked if there were any meaningless numbers printed small on those forged bills of sale he'd just laid hands on.

Vail looked, nodded, and replied with a shrug, "They's always meaningless gobbledygook small print on government forms. I suspect they throw it in to make 'em look officious."

Longarm shook his head and said, "You tell him, Henry."

Henry shot him a grateful look and told Vail, "I suspect they may mean something to the Government Printing Office, sir. With just such events in mind, Washington may designate different shipments to different posts in some sort of numerical code."

Vail brightened and asked, "Are you saying it might be possible to trace just which Army office these blank forms were lifted from, Henry?"

When Henry said that was about the size of it, Vail asked, "Why are you just standing there, Henry? Get your skinny ass out of here and wire Washington!"

As their tall pale clerk lit out, Vail turned to Longarm to ask him, "What are *you* waiting for? A kiss goodbye?"

Longam nodded soberly and replied, "After you tell me where I'm off to, sweetheart."

Vail shrugged and said, "Ain't certain, yet. Go home and pack for your field mission whilst I figure where in the field I mean to send you. And for Gawd's sake change them pants. You smell like a combination of a wet sheep and a dying pony!"

Longarm rose to his considerable height, allowing his prissy tweeds were overdue a stay at the dry cleaners in any case. He knew better than to say how he meant to dress for the field. For if old Billy Vail had no way of knowing he was in violation of their dress code, old Billy would never have to account for his senior deputy looking less officious.

But before he left, Longarm asked, "What about the one and original Jefferson Boyd? I was figuring on seeing if I could get him to sing us a song, after I'd let him pace a piece."

Vail said, "He ain't paced enough, yet. Go on home and change into your cowboy suit and let your four o'clock shadow ripen, some. For I swear when you're all sun-faded denim and stubble you scare *me*!"

It was widely held around the federal building you had to get up mighty early to put one over on Billy Vail.

Longarm chuckled and lit out for his furnished digs on the less fashionable side of Cherry Creek. Once he got there he changed into the clean but faded work duds his boss had cited, strapping the same gun rig around his lean hips below his denim jacket. He left his work shirt be but swapped the shoestring tie for a knotted bandana. There was no call to change his boots or telescope Stetson.

He drew his Winchester '73 saddle gun from its boot on

the McClellen Army saddle draped over the foot of his bed and loaded the tubular magazine with fifteen of the same S&W .44–40 rounds his revolver carried five to the wheel. A man who left a loaded rifle just laying around or loaded all six chambers of his six-gun was too green to be allowed to be chummy with guns. The same thinking applied to considerations of a live round in the chamber of his saddle gun before he was fixing to fire it serious.

Leaving his saddle and saddle gun be for the moment, Longarm balled his three-piece tweed outfit up in one bundle and locked up to tote his load far as the nearest dry cleaners. When they told him he could have his suit back, cleaned and pressed, come Monday, Longarm assured them there was no hurry. He felt no call to add his suit would keep as well on their hands than in his closet, with him not wearing it.

By then it was going on noon. So Longarm stoked his furnace with hot tamales and chicken enchiladas, followed by tuna pie and black coffee at the Mex joint near the Denver Jail before he drifted over to see if Jefferson Boyd felt like explaining those six horses of a different color.

But when he got there the head turnkey said Boyd *wasn't* there. When Longarm inquired where he might be if he wasn't in jail, the Denver lawman soberly replied, "County morgue."

Longarm almost asked a dumb question before he asked, "What might he have died from?"

The head turnkey shrugged and said, "They're still working on it over to the morgue. It wasn't us. Nobody here laid a hand on him. They just found him on his bunk, dead as a turd in a milk bucket, when they went to gather up his breakfast tray a while ago."

Chapter 5

Longarm knew his way to and around the Denver Morgue. So they knew him and it saved a powwow out front.

Thanks to taking his time at that Mex joint, they'd about finished the autopsy when he strode in to join them. He was just as glad. Naked bodies cut open on a slab were unsettling even when they were frogs. But they'd put everything back in and proceeded to stitch up the big Y-shaped incision with butcher's twine by then.

The head of the forensics team knew Longarm of old and didn't ask what he was there for. He said, "Strychnine. Don't need toxicology tests with wolf poison. The effects are dramatic. Three ways he might have wound up full of the nasty shit. If he took it himself he didn't know much about strychnine. The convulsions have been known to break the victim's spine. In his case it was close, but no cigar."

Longarm asked what the other two choices might be.

The medical examiner replied, "The bread and beans the county served for breakfast or the paid-for grub prisoners with pocket-jingle are allowed to send out for. Hard to wolf poison a pot of beans without killing everybody in the cell block. They'd know at the jail who took his order for waffles with maple syrup and link sausages."

Longarm almost asked how they knew what the victim had eaten for breakfast. But he never did, and allowed he'd find out at the nearby lock-up how a prosperous horse trader might have enjoyed such a tempting last meal.

That turned out easy. He was told at the front desk the waitress known as Ruby from the beanery across the way had taken his order and brought Boyd's breakfast back to his cell an hour later. He hadn't wanted and hadn't been served Denver's offer of bread and beans. But after that the waitress known as Ruby was well-known around the jailhouse and had never poisoned any prisoners before.

Longarm thanked the desk to amble out and across to the beanery they directed him to. They told him there he'd just missed the waitress known as Ruby. She worked the graveyard shift from just before midnight to just before noon, changing places with a waitress who served the noon diners. The friendly enough Greek they both worked for said the waitress known as Ruby might have gone home to her furnished digs in a nearby rooming house, if she hadn't headed off to that stock show or gone sight-seeing somewhere else. Ruby was fairly new in town.

But when Longarm asked how new the Greek conceded she'd been in Denver since Easter, at least. Longarm knew Greeks took Easter serious. So he was inclined to believe him.

The Greek wrote her address down in an order pad, tore out the slip and sent Longarm on his way, commencing to feel like a chicken with its head cut off as they ran him in blind circles. But that was why they called it legwork and things could have been worse. He could have been pawing through the files at the office and given his druthers Longarm would as soon pull kitchen police for the Army.

At the rooming house Longarm found the front door

open with a colored gal mopping the hall. When Longarm flashed his badge and told her what he was there for she directed him up the stairs and went back to her chores. Longarm knocked on the door marked B up yonder and when the door opened he saw the waitress known as Ruby had been changing out of her waitress uniform. It was none of his beeswax whether she'd meant to go out or go to bed. As she went on buttoning up he allowed he was sorry to disturb her but they had to talk about the one and original Jefferson Boyd.

The somewhat over-ripe but still handsome henna-rinsed waitress could have lost ten pounds without it hurting her, but thanks to working on her feet twelve hours at a time the effect was more soft-all-over than dumpy. She started to say she didn't know any Jefferson Boyd. Then she proved she had a memory by adding, "Oh, sure, at the jailhouse. I brought his breakfast of . . . let me see . . . waffles with bacon? What about him?"

Longarm said, "He's dead. Wolf poison. And you served him waffles with link sausage, Miss Ruby."

She blanched and said, "I never! Come inside and let me shut this door before you accuse me of murdering paying customers!"

So he stepped in and she not only shut but barrel-bolted the hall door as he tersely brought her up to date on that autopsy.

She sighed and asked, "Does that mean I'm under arrest?"

He shook his head to reply with a smile, "Not hardly. Words exchanged at both the jailhouse and the place you work have led me to suspect you were the unwitting tool of a third party. The victim was being held on suspicion because we suspected he could have told us more than he let on about a ring of interstate horse thieves. I now suspect we must have been right. They didn't want him to tell us what he knew, so they shut him up forever. The poison was likely in the sweet maple syrup. Easier than either the waffles or . . . hold on, might he have ordered tea or coffee with his breakfast?"

She replied without hesitation, "Coffee. I'd remember tea. Do you mind if I shuck this half-shucked waitress uniform? I'm wearing a chemise under it, of course."

He said to go ahead and it turned out you couldn't see all that much more of her when she stripped down to her thinner cotton shimmy shirt.

As she neatly folded and hung up her uniform he got to see more of her arms and legs. But her legs, whilst shapely enough, were encased in black lisle stockings and Longarm had never been one of those faint hearts inspired to jerk off by the sight of exposed arms and shoulders. He found her offer of a French cigarette more thought-provoking, since they'd just met and Her Majesty, Victoria, was said to disapprove of smoking in mixed company. But he was a sport about it, since the offer of a three-for-a-nickel cheroot would have shocked Her Majesty more.

As he lit both their dainty smokes in the center of her one room the waitress known as Ruby sighed and said, "You don't remember me, do you? I try to watch my weight but there's nothing a girl can do about the cruel teeth of time."

He gallantly lied, "I've been trying to recall, Miss Ruby. You wore your hair different, way back when, right?"

She took a defiant drag on her French cigarette and said, "I know henna can be detected by the discerning eye. But who wants to go through life with hair the color of belly button floss? It was in Trinidad near the south state line. Not that long ago, gol durn it. I was slinging hash in the Harvey House and, all right, I was a bottle blonde in those days."

"Oh, sure, it's all coming back to me," he went on lying, even as he took her in his arms. For wherever they'd met in the past there was no mistaking the smoke signals in her big brown eyes.

He kissed her. She kissed back with a French accent. As they came up for air he asked how come she'd left the Harvey House in Trinidad.

She hugged him closer, thrust her pelvis up to press tighter against him, and pouted, "This is why. Like I told you down Trinidad way, Fred Harvey fires girls who get this friendly with his customers."

Longarm hesitated before he made his next expected move. Thanks to an early morning start with Al and Pal out on the outskirts of town, Longarm was not as horny as some might have felt in the company of a henna-rinse-gal-fired-by-the-Harvey-chain-for-acting-horny. After all he was on duty and Miss Lemonade Lucy in Washington would have already been shocked by his violations of the current dress code for federal lawmen on duty.

After all the waitress known as Ruby was a witness, not a suspect, and it was a scientific fact that a relaxed and friendly witness was more likely to dig deeper in his or her filed memories during a pillow conversation. So he kissed her some more, swept her off her feet, and fell across her made-up bedding with her.

"You don't waste much time, do you?" she giggled as he proceeded to shuck her out of that shimmy shirt. He just went on shucking, trying to recall just when and where they'd been in such a friendly position before. He figured they had to have been, from the way she helped when her shimmy shirt got stuck in her henna-rinsed hair on its way off. All she'd had on under it were those black stockings, and they were gartered at mid-thigh. So he had it showing hard and where she wanted it betwixt her welcoming wide-spread naked thighs as she unbuckled his gun belt, saying, "I like a man who's armed and dangerous. But do we really need this *other* dangerous weapon, darling?"

41

He liked a gal who could undress a man and screw like a mink at the same time. So by the time they were both buck naked, save for their socks, Longarm and the waitress known as Ruby felt like old pals indeed.

He waited until they were sharing one of her French cigarettes atop the bedding of her narrow bed—there was a lot to be said for narrow beds at such times—before he brought up the subject of less friendly doings.

She said, "You thought you'd fucked me before, down Trinidad way, didn't you?"

To which he could only reply, "Well, didn't I?"

She pouted "That Jewish girl and our Scotch supervisor saw you first and was I ever jealous. Which of them was better at times like these?"

He calmly replied, "I only had but one of 'em," and never told her which. He said, "Let's talk about recent murders instead of ancient history, Miss Ruby. Did you serve the late Jefferon Boyd on earthenware with cutlery or the disposable paper cups and saucers of your trade?"

She said, "Everything but the stamped tin knife and fork, along with a throw-away can of syrup, was pasteboard. I kept the tray and carried it back with me. Going back for dirty dishes costs time and time is money in the take-out trade."

Snuggling her closer with a generous tit cupped in his free hand, he decided, "I vote for the sweet maple syrup as the murder weapon. The can would have been opened earlier, right?"

She said, "Of course. They don't allow can openers in that cell block. I had his order and . . . let's see, four others, all told, riding on the serving cart I rolled over to the jailhouse and . . ."

"Hold on and back up." He cut in, asking, "Could you swear in court you never took your eyes from that serving cart as you rolled it all over creation during the morning rush hour?"

She said, "Of course not. Would you pinch my nipple harder as you roll it so betwixt your fingers, lover? You sure know how to treat a girl. Where did you learn to strum a girl's banjo as she was hovering on the brink like so?"

He shrugged a bare shoulder against her soft cheek and confessed it had just come to him one afternoon in a hayloft the summer before they'd held that war for him and those other teenagers. He said, "Somebody who knows the routine around that jailhouse . . . Hold on, somebody who knew what his victim was likely to order for breakfast, simply switched cans of syrup most anywhere along the line. Like lots of stage magic, such a trick ain't all that complexicated. Neither you nor anyone else suspected any such switchery was likely. It'd be a waste of time trying to determine exactly where you paused with that cart and looked somewhere else long enough to matter."

She sighed and said, "They could have picked up the one can and put the other down as I was pushing the damned cart, for all the attention I was paying. Have you any idea how bored, bored, bored a poor girl born with a romantic nature can get, pushing a fucking food cart to grubby old men behind bars?"

He replied, "I just now said that. I knew all along you were innocent. Of poisoning customers, I mean. Our incarcerated suspect was done in by another crook who knew his onions. I doubt he left any sign to cut in the neighborhood of that jailhouse. So I reckon we'll have to circle wider to cut his trail."

She asked if they could fornicate some more before he had to leave and he was willing to try, seeing he had no idea what anybody else wanted him to try at the moment.

Thanks to earlier time spent with Al and Pal he suggested dog style so's he could spare his weary spine some effort. For as most folk learn on their honeymoon, if not their first long weekend with a frisky gal, dog style allows the active partner to just shift his weight back and forth as long as he can keep it stiff, and it's easier to keep it stiff when it dosen't take half the effort.

By the same token, being such a slower way to get there, dog style is the best position next to pillow talk for relaxed conversation. So by the time he felt ready to roll her over and finish right Longarm had thoroughly explored the ways of a take-out waitress before he took it out of her with a wistful remark about having to take it on down the pike.

The waitress known as Ruby didn't try to stop him. She wasn't used to such protracted fornication, never having been informed about Al and Pal. So they kissed and parted friendly, once he had his gun back on.

By then the school kids were busting loose across downtown Denver but Longarm made it back to his home office in plenty of time to tell Billy Vail what he'd found out across town, leaving out some parts about a waitress known as Ruby.

Vail said, "We've been busy, too. You and Henry were right about secret codes. All the faked remount papers we have on file were sent to Fort Leavenworth by the Government Printing Office. So Henry has typed up your travel orders. You're to ride the rails to K.C. and board the first steamboat up to Fort Leavenworth."

Longarm demanded, "To what end? We already know somedy swiped a mess of government forms at Fort Leavenworth, if not in Washington, earlier, and the sneak who just murdered a material witness is still at large here in Denver!"

Vail calmly replied, "Denver P.D. can investigate murders in Denver. That's what it's paid to do. Another funny pattern has emerged from the reports from all over. The ring stealing Army mounts and selling them as surplus with forged government bills of sale has to be big as hell if the Army is missing stock from border to border."

"Or a gang of more manageable size that moves around a lot?" Longarm objected.

Vail shrugged and said, "Whatever. That ain't what's so mysterious. What's so mysterious is them six gray horses of another color. All the stolen stock *reported* stolen has been easier to dispose of Army bays. Few days ago somebody sold a *white* charger with suspiciously thoroughbred lines up to Cheyenne, offering the same phoney remount paper."

Longarm said, "Looks like some field grade officer must be missing a parade mount."

Vail nodded but said, "Damned A. Only no field grade officer has reported such a loss. So tell me how come horses of another color keep turning up with forged Army papers if no such horses have been reported stolen!"

"I'd best be on my way to Fort Leavenworth, in the country where they raise such horses." Longarm sighed.

Chapter 6

Colorado had commenced as a westward expanse of Kansas and from the foothills of the Front Range west of Denver to Kansas City on the Big Muddy everything looked much the same, albeit the rolling sea of grass punctuated by wooded draws rolled at ever lower altitude as one rode the rails east and the grass on the windswept crests grew taller. For west of, say, Longitude 100° where you got less rain and homesteaders had no business trying, it had revolved the way Professor Darwin said things did from buffalo to cattle county on the seemingly endless carpet of buffalo, bunch, blue grama and other shortgrasses. So you couldn't grow crops without irrigation, albeit sunflower windmills scattered hither and yon showed how many homesteaders were willing to try.

East of such Kansas cow towns as Dodge to the south or Hays on the K.C. line he was riding they got enough rain for big blue stem and such. With fewer windmills where the water table lay high enough for old-time "wishing wells" out back. It had taken him all afternoon to make it that far east and what you could still see of Kansas out yonder rolled purple and gold under a flamingo sky as the sun went down back up the tracks a ways. Lamplights were winking on in the homesteads as they passed like ships in the night. When they

47

stopped to jerk water at a dinky prairie town a voice behind him observed, "How quaint. Kansas is just as I have always imagined the steppes of Russia in the time of Catherine the Great! I could swear all these identical hamlets were fashioned for her by that crafty prime minister. I forget his name."

"Potemkin, ma'am," said Longarm as he turned to regard the gal in the seat behind him with a denim-clad elbow propped up betwixt them. She sure looked startled.

After that, as far as he could tell by the tricky gloaming light they were rolling through together, she seemed a well-hatted brunette of, say, thirty with a plain but expensive-looking travel duster over whatever she had on under it. As she stared at him thunderghasted, Longarm introduced himself and added, "I read about Queen Catherine and her crafty prime minister in this tome about Russia from the Denver Public Library and I follow your drift about them Potemkin Villages he devised to please Her Somewhat Imperious Majesty. But them Kansas jerkwaters along this line ain't painted canvas theatrical scenery sent on ahead and set up on the sly with actors playing happy peasants to welcome a Prussian queen who never learned a word of Russian. The towns we keep passing all look the same 'cos they were built of pre-cut lumber to the same mail order plans at about the same time."

He twisted to a more comfortable position and added, "As in the case of all them recently conquered Russian steppes, these parts got settled in a bunch, just after the war back east."

She said, "I thought I was talking to myself."

Longarm sighed and said, "Then we'll say no more about it. I know how it gets, riding along for hours with nobody to talk to but your ownself. I understand you ain't in trouble 'til you start to hear answers."

She laughed and said, "I just did, and I must say it gave me a turn. Forgive my manners, Deputy Long. I am Penelope Mansfield of Twelvetrees Plantation out of Kennesaw, or I used to be. You see, Kennesaw is just outside Atlanta and when Sherman marched to the sea . . ."

"My friends call me Custis and I never rid with Sherman." Longarm cut in to spare them both the mournful dirge. He added, "I disremember which side I fought for. It was all so long ago, and we all had a lot of growing up to do."

She took the broad hint and dimpled. "My friends call me Penny. Now that I've given you a second glance I can see you are a gentleman of some education . . . Custis. It's just that on first glance I took you for . . ."

"A cowboy. Unemployed." Longarm answered easily, brushing some of the fly ash from the locomotive stack ahead off his sleeve as he went on to explain, "I reckon I ought to buy me a travel duster one of these days but I don't spend all that much time aboard trains and the oil cloth rain slicker lashed to my saddle up above gets too hot and sweaty when it ain't raining."

She assured him she understood there was much to be said for traveling in work duds if one had them. He knew she didn't. He didn't care to hear how she'd been getting by since they'd lost the old plantation and other glories of the Old South in The War Between The States.

You never said Civil War in the presence of a Southern Lady. •

She asked if he was going on to Kansas City. He tried not to sound too wistful as he replied, "Almost. Got to get off at a jerkwater called Jubilee Junction to consult the local law about a horse of another color."

She blinked in an amused way and asked, "Custis, is what you just said supposed to make a lick of sense?"

He explained, "Blacksmith in Jubilee Junction came by a snow white officer's charger wearing the brand of the U.S. Army Remount Service. He said he got it in exchange for putting a whole bunch of sold off Army bays back on new shoes. A local deputy who used to ride with the 10th Cav had a suspicious look at the critter. Its bill of sale gives its age as say seven or eight. Its teeth describe it as a four-year-old in its prime. That's all we got on the wire as I was fixing to leave Denver, earlier today. Figured I'd spend some time in Jubilee Junction as long as it's not out of my way."

That inspired her to ask more about his mission and seeing anything was more inspiring to talk about than Sherman's March To The Sea they were still discussing the mystery over supper in the dining car ahead when Longarm treated his fellow traveler to a meal, even if he'd never have her for dessert. Gents who were only kind to others when they meant to get something out of it were not exactly gents in Longarm's book.

As she put her own mind to it, Penny suggested, "What if those high-toned officers' mounts were never reported stolen because they were never stolen? What if they were simply sold by embarrassed officers to pay off gambling debts or, well, play-pretties for some . . . friends their wives might not know about, or understand? Hasn't it been widely rumored General Custer had a Cheyenne mistress on the side?"

Helping himself to more chicken à la King, that was what they called it on the menu, Longarm thoughtfully replied, "He was only a lieutenant colonel and he never sold his horse for any gal of any complexion. I've always taken that Cheyenne gal with a grain of salt. That story they tell about the Indians respecting his remains was a whopper made up to comfort his widow, Miss Libbie. They were said to have adored each other and he got in trouble more than once, going A.W.O.L. to be with her. But old George had heaps of personal enemies inclined to question his habit of questioning Indian policy and you just don't know who to believe about a man who ain't here to defend himself."

He chewed whatever in thunder was on his fork, decided it was safe to swallow, and added, "As to that Miss Monahseetah some say he was seeing on the side, reporters looking to interview her can't seem to find her. Officers defending their own courage against Custer's say Monahsee-

50

tah is up in Canada with the rest of her nation. If she is, that makes Cheyenne more forgiving than most. I don't know you well enough to repeat what Mexicans say about the Indian mistress of Mister Cortez."

She dimpled and suggested it seemed a shame they'd never get to know one another that well. Gals killing time aboard a ship or railroad train tended to talk bold, knowing nobody was going to be able to take 'em up on it.

And so the conversation went as they wound up back in the club car after supper, with both of them sipping soft drinks because Kansas had just gone dry and the laws were enforced east of Hays.

So they both knew she was cold sober when Longarm fished out his watch and declared he had to go forward and gather up his baggage as he'd be getting off at Jubilee Junction and she allowed she was getting off with him.

As she tagged along, Penny explained, "I know you must be shocked by my forward manner, Custis. I know I am. But I can't bear the thought of never knowing how your visit to the Potemkin Village ahead turns out!"

He chuckled as he held a door betwixt cars open for her but warned her, "Sometimes it can take days to check out a report. With nights in between, if you follow my drift."

Seeing they were face to face, alone betwixt cars, Penny kissed him, bold as brass, before she demurely replied, "I follow your drift and I mean to follow you off this train at Jubilee Junction. So we better see about my carpetbag, as well!"

They did. It only took betting the porter a quarter he couldn't have his saddle and her bag handy by the time they rolled in to the junction.

They kissed a dozen times more out on the platform by the time the train had stopped. The grinning porter helped them down to the sun-baked open loading platform. There was nobody on the same at that hour. But as they saw light in the nearby ticket office and waiting room of a hip-roofed

51

shed across the platform Longarm picked up all their baggage to lead the way.

He heard Penny suck in her breath as they entered what seemed all the action in such a dinky dry town at that hour. The waiting room wasn't all that crowded. Two older gents were having a spirited game of checkers at a table in the center of the waiting room. Other men and a couple of local women were gathered around to watch and one gathered the game was being played for money. Everyone froze in place like the figures in a wax museum tableau as Longarm and Penny entered. Not even the air seemed to be moving as everyone held their breath.

Longarm said, "Evening, folks. I'd be U.S. Deputy Custis Long and I'm looking for your marshal Brown?"

One of the frozen figures managed, graciously enough, "Marshal's office jess across the square to the north, suh."

There came a murmur of agreement. Longarm thanked them all and craw-fished back outside with Penny and their baggage, saying, "May as well circle around."

She said, "Custis, everyone in there was a *darky*!"

Longarm said, "I noticed. We seem to be in one of those colored towns set up out this way for freed slaves by Pap Singleton, a Tennessee carpenter they call a Black Moses. He founded this resettlement society out our way for folk who no longer felt welcome in Dixie."

She sniffed, "Or vice versa! Dosen't it make your flesh crawl, knowing we must be the only white folk in town tonight?"

He soothed, "Aw, there's always some of everything in every town. If there ain't no other white folk here, what of it? Were you fixing to start a race riot?"

She shuddered and said, "I certainly hope not. But did you see the *looks* some of them gave us back there, Custis? I don't know how I'm supposed to act around darkies. *Free* darkies, I mean. I always got along fine with our . . . *help* before the Damnyankees put ideas in their heads."

Longarm suggested, "You'd best just keep still and let me do the talking, then. I never got to boss around much . . . *help* back in West-By-God-Virginia and since then I've noticed most folk meet you halfways if you let 'em."

He led the way across the leaf-littered square of still-green grass to where a lamplit sign above a door declared the place the office of the town law.

Inside, as no surprise, they found the night man on duty a gentleman of color. Neither he nor Longarm saw any need to comment on this as they established Marshal Brown would be back around eight in the morning.

Longarm said, "Wanted to talk with him and others in town during regular business hours, anyway. Got in late in answer to his wire because that's the way the K.C. Lone runs. Might you all have a hotel here in Jubilee Junction, pard?"

The deputy hesitated, not looking directly at the white gal at Longarm's side as he replied, "More than one . . . traveling saleman passing through has stayed at the Sweet Chariot Hotel just up Main Street and never filed no complaints with us, Deputy Long."

So Longarm thanked him, said they'd give her a try, and left with Penny and their baggage.

Outside, she marveled, "That wasn't awkward as I'd feared it might be. You sure have a way with darkies, Custis. You talked to that colored boy like he was a white man and had I closed my eyes I'd have taken it for a normal conversation betwixt fellow lawmen!"

He said, "We are fellow lawmen. He was wearing a badge. Talking to another man ain't no big deal unless somebody makes a big deal of it."

She asked, "What if he'd been, you know, upitty?"

Longarm said, "I've had upittied him right back. But I try not to cross such a bridge before I come to it. There'd be less trouble in this world if we all waited to see if surly manners might be called for."

"Are you saying you never run into surly manners, Custis?" she asked.

He sighed and said, "Happens all the time. Cliches get to be cliches because they're sometimes simple facts. There *are* Upitty Coons, Drunken Irishmen, Thieving Mexicans and Wild Indians. Still makes more sense to make the hand sign for 'Howdy' when you meet up with strange Indians on the lone prairie. Most folk, say nine out of ten folk, are hoping against hope you don't get upitty with *them*."

The desk clerk at the Sweet Chariot Hotel was darker but more polished than the town deputy who commended the establishment. When Longarm acted the same as he'd have acted checking into any hotel the desk clerk acted a tad more refined than some desk clerks and had a black bell-hop in a crisp maroon uniform take their baggage up to the room with bath Longarm had asked for. High-toned hotels never asked to see a marriage license. When a whore looked like a whore they didn't have a vacancy.

As soon as they were alone upstairs, Penny marveled, "Heavens, this suite seems as clean and tidy as any white hotel!"

As Longarm hung up his hat he asked, "Why shouldn't it? Who did you think they have cleaning the rooms in *most* hotels, Eskimo seal hunters?"

She blinked and said, "You know, you're right. Back at Twelvetrees my mama was a house-proud hostess who couldn't abide a speck of dust. But now that I think back, we were never the ones who dusted!"

She laughed like a kid swiping apples as she unpinned her hat and shucked her travel duster, to reveal a summer-weight frock of thin ecru pongee she'd sweated some.

Turning her back to Longarm, she demurely asked if he'd mind undoing the buttons down her back, sounding sort of throaty as she added, "Lord knows where following you through darkest Africa is likely to lead little old me, for I'm already starting to feel so . . . *primitive* around you!"

Chapter 7

Longarm was young, healthy and used to hard riding. But he'd mounted four women in less than twenty-four hours so he was having a tough time in the love saddle of Penny Mansfield. But she took it as a compliment as he kept plugging away and it helped that she was built way different than the waitress known as Ruby.

Penny was firmer of flesh and longer of limb with the trim hips of a gal who'd had her own pony as a kid. It hardly seemed fair but it seemed true that gals who'd grown up rich wound up with better shapes as time and labor tore at them. Provided a rich gal wasn't a chocolate-stuffing lazybones, the aristocratic pursuits of horseback riding or tennis and such firmed a woman up without making her firm than pounding laundry or scrubbing floors on her knees, long past feeling weary, might. Rich gals got to quit and sip iced tea once they'd felt they'd glowed enough for now. Bathing regular with castile soap followed by lotions and such kept their hides soft and smooth long past the time it took poor working gals to toughen up. So Penny was still in her prime and knew it. She said she wanted him to leave the bed lamp lit because she was afraid of the dark with darkies all around. He never asked if she'd left a night-light burning behind a locked bedroom door back on the Twelvetrees Plantation. He prefered to think she was proud of her ass instead of ashamed of her past.

He rode on to glory by not trying too hard as he posted in her love saddle and just enjoyed the ride without trying for any brass rings and so they just got to know one another in the Biblical sense. He suddenly found himself fixing to come and, from the way she was thrusting up to meet him, Penny was getting there, too.

He slowed down to give her more time and, human privates being so perverse, the holding back resulted in a raging lust a man in his position had no call to feel.

But it sure felt great, all the way down to his curled-under toes, as they both climaxed in a shudder of sheer delight.

As they lay there entwined like head-shot snakes, Penny softly asked if he'd wake her up when they came to bury her. Seeing she'd just died and gone to heaven. He didn't answer. He was too contented to purr.

After a time, of course, they wound up sharing one of his cheroots because she hadn't packed any tobacco along. She said some of the ladies in her circle dipped snuff, but that she cottoned to real smoking or none at all. He never said he'd noticed she seemed a woman who took physical pleasures all or nothing. It might have seemed rude and he had not one complaint about the way she'd taken charge of thier love life, Lord love her.

As they lay there smoking Penny suddenly decided, "Those horses of a different color will lead us to the answer."

He blinked and said, "Come again?"

Penny said, "I mean to, in a little while," as she took his limp, no longer virile member in her free hand, adding, "I meant those white or gray mounts neither stolen nor sold off by that Remount Service you told me about seem the weakest links in the chain of evidence. Those plain old brown horses stolen for certain in greater numbers should have records tangled as a rat's nest and I fear it would take forever to trace each and every one back to where it was bred, when the Remount Service bought it, where it was sent from that Fort Leavenworth and so on."

Longarm said, "Mayhaps not forever. But this child ain't looking forward to that much paperwork."

She asked, "How many horses of a different color might we be talking about, darling?"

He thought before he admitted, "Ain't certain. No more than a dozen, so far, I reckon."

She snuggled closer and said, "Even if each has a different story to tell, there aren't as many to track down."

He started to ask a dumb question. But he nodded and said, "I follow your drift. One or more might have been sold off on the sly by a needy officer. Officers buy their own mounts, even when they buy them off the Remount Service. So they feel free to dispose of them as they see fit and a squadron commander with expensive gambling debts might not see fit to advertise 'em."

He took another drag and added, "Other owners of parade mounts might have other motives. Once you consider the ways an officer or any other gent with a horse of his own to sell might need to sell it, sudden and on the sneak . . . But hold on, Miss Penny. Them suspicious horses of another color were all sold, or appeared to be sold, with a forged Remount Service bill of sale. Faked service records with made up signatures of nonexistant Remount Officers."

She suggested, "Well, if someone wanted to sell his own horse in a discreet manner . . ."

"Using the same government blanks, encoded for delivery to the Remount Depot at Fort Leavenworth by the Government Printing Office?" he cut in.

She sighed and said, "You're right. It's too mysterious for me. Could I get on top, now?"

Longarm snuffed the cheroot and found to his pleased surprise that she could. He didn't ask how she'd gotten it up for him. Considering her aristocratic airs, Penny would have made a swell milkmaid. Or at any rate a gal who'd given a hell of a heap of swell hand jobs. No man with a lick of sense ever asked a gal where she'd learned such tricks for gals tended to tell them and once a gal got to "confessing" it tended to turn into bragging.

But thanks to however she'd gotten so skilled with her dainty hands he was soon doing her right with a pillow under her rolicking rump and her ankles locked about the nape of his neck whilst she accused him of trying to kill her until he offered to take it easier and she told him she'd kill him if he dared.

He suspected she had by the time she allowed him to trim the lamp so's they could try for some shut-eye.

Once the hotel room was plunged in darkness she snuggled closer and complained she was edgy about the darkies all around.

He wrapped a comforting arm around her bare shoulders as he soothed, "Miss Penny, shiftless shuffling watermelon thieves seldom come out west to carve new lives out of an unforgiving land."

She sniffed, "Then why do they scare me so? Back home before the war I was never scared of the . . . help. And we had more than some."

He suggested, "Mayhaps it's because the colored folk out our way ain't *property*. Lots of Sotherons seem uncertain around folk who still *look* like property but may say or do most anything they please. Like I said, me and mine never took part in the Peculiar Institution so we don't feel as peculiar around freed slaves."

She said, "People of quality never called them slaves. We regarded our help as family and they respected us in turn."

Longarm wanted to go to sleep. So he knew better than to question how some members of a "Family" might feel about chopping cotton whilst other "Family" members sipped mint juleps on the veranda. West-By-God-Virginia had hived off the onetime larger Old Virginia with a view to avoiding such "Family Matters." The mountainous western counties hadn't supported the lifestyles of the Tidewater plantation folk. As in the case of rocky New England or even the thrifty farmlands of the Pennsylvania Dutch, the hills of his boyhood hadn't encouraged slave holding, so nobody had held many slaves.

In the morning, after breakfast in bed served by a cheerful colored gal who seemed to "know her place" according to Penny, she was willing to hold the fort, slugabed, while he tended to his business in town.

Marshal Brown turned out to be a hefty gentleman of color sporting a tin star with no chip on his shoulder. Both lawmen understood they were working with a horse of another color as they talked about those horses of another color. But neither had call to mention it. So neither did.

As Brown led the way to the smithy of one Walter Lewis, Longarm was able to bring him up to date on things he hadn't known about the case, albeit by now most every lawman across the land knew somebody was surely stealing a whole lot of Army horses.

When Brown asked if Longarm knew how come they were trying to sell younger stolen mounts as surplus stock worth so much less, Longarm told him, "Two reasons. To begin with it's generally known you can't buy a horse wearing an Army brand unless it's over seven years old and after that a so-called surplus mount with the teeth of a critter in its prime is sure to be snapped up fast with fewer questions asked. A bargain is a bargain and you know what they say about looking a gift horse in the mouth."

Brown objected, "They still ain't getting half the price of a new Army bay."

To which Longarm replied, "Mayhaps not. But they've been gettin' sixty or more sudden, by the gross, and we're talking in circles, pard."

By then they'd made it the smithy, where Walter Lewis

turned out a shade lighter in complexion and darker in mood.

As Brown tried to introduce their white visitor Lewis complained in a belligerant tone, "Why you bring this *ofey* fool here, fool? I tole you I never stole that fucking white horse from any white cocksucker!"

Brown warned, "Watch you mouth, nigger!"

Longarm sighed and said, "Nobody here has any call for a chip on his shoulder, gents. Nobody's accused anybody of stealing any horse, Mister Lewis. We haven't even managed to prove it was stolen in the first place from anybody."

The burly blacksmith asked in a more curious tone, "What you talking 'bout, ah . . . lawman? Didn't this badge toting he-coon tell me that white horse I took in payment was a stolen Army mount?"

Longarm explained, "He meant it *looked* to be a stolen Army mount. A three- or four-year-old with an Army brand. After that nobody's reported it missing. Where might it be right now?"

"Ask this know-it-all!" pounted Lewis, waving the hammer in his fist at the local law.

Brown said, "We've impounded it. As evidence. Pending some idea who the hell it was stolen from!"

The smith demanded, "Who means to pay me for all them other brutes I shod if I can't sell that one fucking horse?"

Longarm said, "Don't give up the ship just yet, Mr. Lewis. As I read the law, any rightful owner of an impounded apparently ownerless critter has ninety days to come foreward and claim it. After which, said critter becomes the lawful property of whoever found it."

Marshal Brown objected, "This upitty country boy never *found* that white charger, Deputy Long. You just heard him say he took it as payment for aiding and abetting!"

Longarm shook his head and replied, "As payment for honest toil, yes. Aiding and abetting, no. The crooks who stuck him with a mysterious horse of another color and a phoney bill of sale never *told* him they'd slipped him a wooden nickel, or a horse he'd never be able to sell. So he's on *our* side. Ain't that right, Walt?"

Walter Lewis said, "Well, *sure* that's right! I's been . . . *victimated* by them horse thieves and what was that about ninety days, Mr. Lawman?"

Longarm said, "Seeing the horse was left on these premises by a person or persons unknown, and seeing you are the owner of this property, it's the same as if they abandoned or lost it on your property. So unless it proves to be a stolen horse it's a *lost* or *stray* horse in the eyes of the law, if you follow my drift."

They both laughed. Brown said, "There you go, Walt. We'll hold your horse for you ninety days and if nobody comes forward it'll be your horse. Fair enough?"

The mollified smith allowed it was. So Longarm got out his notebook and they got to work on descriptions.

Walter Lewis recalled the four white riders who'd stopped by to have those horses reshod, mayhaps to make it tougher to track them, as four white men dressed for fall riding in denim and sheepskin with regular broad-brimmed hats of no distinguishing shape or style. On reflection he recalled two of them had mustaches and two were smooth shaven. Longarm told him he'd been a big help.

As Brown walked him back toward the town square Brown told him he was sorry that was all the fool smith had been able to come up with.

Longarm said, "I meant what I said. A vague description is better than none. My boss calls what we were just up to the process of eliminating. We just eliminated Indians, Mexicans, women or children. At least four members of the ring are nonedescript white riders. Nondescript can be a description in itself. We've eliminated hunchbacks, dwarves or giants. Could I have a look at that white horse, now?"

Brown allowed he sure could and led him past the

square and across the tracks, where a corner of their stock-yards had been declared a pound with one ownerless critter impounded in the same.

The white standardbred gelding had been watered and foddered earlier that morning. But it must have gotten lonely overnight because when it saw the two lawmen approaching it pricked up its ears and when Longarm called it came over to the rails with a friendly snort.

Longarm cupped its friendly muzzle in his left hand, softly saying, "Well, sure you're a good old hoss! You want to show your teeth to one who loves the shit out of you, old hoss?"

The young gelding wasn't too sure about that but Longarm got a grip on its lubbering lips and pried its mouth open to remark, "Son of a bitch this one's five years old! How do you figure that Army brand, Marshal Brown?"

Brown suggested, "Somebody branded him? I told your office in that wire someone left an Army horse on our hands with one of those phoney bills of sale made out as if by the Army Remount Service. You want to see that, too? Got it over to the office."

Longarm said, "Not hardly. Got a train and then a steamboat to catch today. The numbers you copied for us match those on all the other phoney government paper. Phoney writing on real government forms, I mean."

As he turned the white gelding loose with a friendly caress Brown shook his head and said, "I can't say what I'm missing. But I must be missing *something*. 'Cause I can't make a lick of sense of all this hogwash, Deputy Long! Can you?"

Longrm soberly replied, "Not hardly. That's how come me and another pal have that train to catch!"

Chapter 8

As the tracks perforce wound down some to the lower flood plain of the Big Muddy, the erosions of many a year made the scenery outside seem like foothill country and the long grass prairie of unsettled stretches was replaced by wooded patches of mostly cottonwood, the tree that won the west.

Found in scattered groves or gallery forests from border to border betwixt the Rockies and the Cumberlands, the substantial cottonwood was kin to the poplar but grew as if it thought it was an elm. Its soft knot-free wood was white as cotton and gave the tree its name. Druthered by Mex wood carvers who fashioned most everything from saddle trees to statuettes of saints from it, cottonwood was more likely to serve as firewood for steamboats forging up and downstream betwixt cottonwood lined banks. Massive cottonwoods that fell into western rivers before they could be cut for firewood formed most of the deadly snags and sawyers out to rip the guts out of unwary steamboats. Growing alongside railroad tracks in autumn in knee-deep fallen leaves, the graceful bare branched cottonwoods just looked pretty 'til they were replaced by helter skelter cornfields with the dry cornstalks shucked and bundled to stand like shaggy soldiers fixing to march off on some winter campaign. And then they were in the outskirts of K.C. which didn't extend that far from the river to the east.

Kansas City lay on the edge of Kansas more than it lay *in* the same. Kansas City, Missouri, lay just across the river to the northeast. K.C. as it was mostly called, had been named back in '36 because the Kansas River that Kansas was named after met the bigger Missouri there in a confusion of swamps they were still working out. The main dry parts of K.C. were downstream of the confusion.

Their train was still rolling when Penny asked how soon their steamboat would be leaving for Fort Leavenworth. Longarm managed a poker face as he allowed Henry's travel orders suggested *he* go direct from the railroad station to the river landings to board the *Creole Dancer* early as she waited there a spell to take on goods and passengers bound upstream.

When she demurely asked if they'd have a stateroom Longarm patted her knee fondly and explained, "Fort Leavenworth ain't but twenty miles or so upstream from K.C., Miss Penny. Henry, the office hand I told you about, figures less than four hours on the water if it's running flood stage."

She said, "But we may well be in port an hour or more and think of the things we could try, by broad day, in a cozy little stateroom for two, if we had even one whole hour to work with!"

He did. It was easier after some time aboard the train to rest up. But tempting as her offer was, Longarm was starting to wonder just how far his long-limbed fellow traveler meant to travel with him.

It wasn't as if he was tired of her long limbs already. As she'd just reminded him, there were heaps of positions they'd never gotten around to yet. On the other hand he was starting to see how some gals might be feeling when they pouted they were being *taken for granted*.

Men and women said mighty goofy things to one another in the process of orgasm. But he couldn't recall having offered to take her along on a field mission. He was allowed to claim travel expenses if and when he got back alive. Sometimes the accounting office even approved some. But he had his doubts about filing for twice the usual expenses and it was commencing to look as if any man traveling with Penny was going to run up expenses no man traveling alone would dream of. Starting with staterooms booked for four-hour river runs.

Penny leaned closer to cite a naughty naughty she'd only read about but had always wanted to try, with the right lover. And seeing they could have the showdown at Fort Leavenworth as well as anywhere else, Longarm decided it was as sensible to hire a stateroom for four hours as a hotel room for a lunch hour. He didn't want to hear how many lunch hour affairs the obviously experienced Penny had managed in her time. It wasn't fair to expect gals you . . . lunched with to have had less experience than your own horny self. Even though that was the way most folk might have druthered.

So when they got off at K.C. and caught a hack to the riverside he was a sport and suggested she mind their baggage near the head of the gangway whilst he scouted up the purser to see about hiring them that coziness.

The *Creole Dancer* was a double deck side-wheeler a tad smaller than one saw on the Mississippi but still a substantial vessel decorated to resemble a floating wedding cake. At the purser's office a clerk told him the officer he wanted to see was up on the passenger deck, having it out with a couple who should have got off a couple stops down-stream or paid more damned passage.

As Longarm went up the stairs to the passenger deck a couple of passengers with some buttons unbuttoned were coming down the same, with the gal fussing at her male escort. Up on the passenger deck Longarm met an older gent with PURSER in gold across the front of his peaked cap and stopped him to ask if he might hire a stateroom.

The purser said, "Just so happens we're changing the linens and sweeping out the remains of a honeymoon at this very moment. Come along with me and I'll show you. How far upstream are we talking about?"

When Longarm told him the older man cocked a brow and said, "We might be able to work a . . . private deal out. What if you were to bet me a buck I couldn't find you and the lady a stateroom and neither of us ever made extra work for the company bookkeepers?"

Longarm allowed that sounded fair to him and the older man led the way aft as, heading the other way, a page boy in a white jacket came shouting, "Call for Mrs. Westfield! Call . . . for . . . Mrs. Westfield!"

It would have sounded dumb to observe somebody had to be looking for a Mrs. Westfield, so Longarm never did. When they got to the stateroom in question the male colored chambermaid had repaired the damages and was airing things out. Longarm felt a certain tingle in his loins as he eyed the fresh-made berth and lost his bet.

As the purser pocketed the silver cartwheel Longarm retraced his steps to tell Penny Mansfield the good news. But when he got to where he'd left her and their baggage only the baggage was there.

Figuring she'd gone aft to heed a call to nature, Longarm leaned on the railing and lit a cheroot. He only commenced to wonder when he saw he'd smoked her down all the way.

He lit another. After he'd smoked *that* down all the way he commenced to worry. But someone would have surely said something had any passengers of either gender fallen overboard.

That same page boy came along the cargo deck, calling out, "All ashore who's going ashore! All ashore who's going ashore!"

Longarm stopped him to ask if he'd ever found that

Mrs. Westfield somebody had asked him to page. The kid replied, "I ain't certain. It was a *Mr.* Westfield who wanted her paged. He was standing right about here. Said they'd told him at the train station his wife had left in a numbered hack and the hack driver had told him he'd delivered her here. So I told him to wait whilst I paged her. I paged her on this deck, I paged her on the passenger deck, I paged her on the Texas deck, to no avail. So he went looking himself. It's allowed, as long as you get off before we leave the landing."

Longarm fished out some pocket jingle with a curious smile. The page boy boy confided, "He was up on the passenger deck when this lady in a travel duster and fashionable hat darted ashore like she was in a hurry. I never asked if she was Mrs. Westfield."

"Might she have sported a dead bluebird on that hat?" asked Longarm.

The kid said, "She surely did. Might you have known her?"

Longarm handed him four bits and said, "Not as well as I thought and what about her husband?"

The kid more than earned his four bits by saying, "About your age. Not as big. Dressed like a banker who rides. Smooth shaven and that's about it. He left without tipping me for paging her. So I felt no call to tell him she might have gone ashore. You reckon she had call to duck her man like so?"

Longarm smiled thinly and replied, "I suspect *he'd* have said so. I reckon I'll hang on to her carpetbag, in the unlikely case she comes back for it."

A colored deckhand offered to relieve Longarm of the heavy McClellan saddle and Longarm let him, tipping him a dime at the door of the now somewhat pointless statetroom.

But at least the privacy provided by the bolted door allowed a right bemused lawman to investigate the mysterious Penny Mansfield or likely Westfield's carpetbag.

There was nothing unmentionalble nor worth mention to be found among all the crumpled-up newspapers she'd packed the bag with. The days old newprint had been published by the *News*, the *Post*, or the *Trib* in Denver. That didn't tell him much. He'd never figured she'd board his train from Denver in Paris, France.

"You were fixing to run off with me before we ever met," Longarm decided. Since nothing else made better sense. Smiling witsfully down into wadded newsprint, Longarm muttered, "Had you told me you were on the run from a husband you feared we might have worked things out better, Penny. Remember what that Scotch poet warned about weaving tangled webs as we set out to bullshit everybody?"

He started to shut the carpetbag with a view to giving it to some deserving crew member. Then he spied the lush label sewed to the watered silk lining near the clasp and recognized it as that of a fancy shop near the opera house he'd visited one time, in the company of a miner's widow who could afford the best and only accepted the best, save for him, as she'd teased.

He shrugged and said, "Well, we knew you looked rich before you ever said you were, Penny. I wonder if there ever was a Twelvetrees Plantation and why in blue blazes I'm wondering. You were out to run away with the first man who'd run away with you and I sure thank you for the running we enjoyed together whilst it lasted. So good hunting and good luck with that cuss you're running away from. For he seems to be a good tracker as well as a bad husband!"

He warned himself it was none of his beeswax how much travel Penny was packing in her purse. He told himself not to worry about a gal who could sure take care of herself and any man lucky enough to be in her company.

He was still thinking about her as the *Creole Dancer* backed off the landing and swung her blunt bows upstream.

Lounging atop the bedding and enjoying another smoke,

Longarm asked his cheroot if it had ever heard tell of that Russian Brotherhood Of The Ants.

The Brotherhood Of The Ants, to hear Russian peasants tell it, was a better way to get rich than the Irish notion of catching a leprechaun.

You didn't have to track down and nab any Russian sprites to join The Brotherhood Of The Ants. The ants who accepted you as a brother were natural ants who, poking about underground all day long, stumbled over specks of gold, bitty diamonds and such. So, seeing no ant had any use for gold or gemstones, they'd bring it to your place and leave it on your doorstep. Seeing you had more use for such riches and seeing they regarded you as a brother.

The way you joined the Brotherhood Of The Ants, as Russian folklore went, was by passing one simple magic test of your sincerity. Ants being mind readers as well as gold miners, they only asked that you go out in the woods alone, sit on a stump for no more than one hour, during which hour you would never, once, picture a big Russian bear in your head.

It sounded easier until you studied on it some. But Russian peasants had said it was easier to walk on water or raise the dead.

He was still thinking about Penny, and big Russian bears, when they landed at suppertime. The military reserve was a brisk walk inland.

Founded back in '27 the erstwhile Headquarters of the Army Of The West had matured into a bewilderment of rear echelon support outfits from distributing new recruits, new livestock, quartermaster and ammuniton supplies and so forth down to the dreaded "Jefferson Barracks" or federal prison known to civilian as well as military criminals as Leavenworth Prison. From the fort to the river a shantytown of frame whorehouses and such, described as "Hog Farms" by the Provost Marshal and ignored as long as they treated off duty soldiers right, were being crowded out by the civilian housing of more respectable "Feather Merchants" the military dismissed as locals they weren't too clear about. Many married or shacked up enlisted men, along with some junior officers, rented uncertainly recorded quarters off the post and at the rate things were going Fort Leavenworth was threatening to turn into a *town* of Leavenworth.

Wanting to feel free to shift his weight as he saw fit, Longarm booked a hotel room near the landing to store his baggage and await his later pleasure before he saw about supper at a riverside shack describing itself as a French restaurant. Folk along the river headed down to New Orleans put on French airs upstream past Des Moins. Longarm figured that was fair. Before that Louisiana Purchase, everything out this way that hadn't been Spanish had been French. Unless it had been Indian, of course. Kansas was named after Sioux-Hokan speakers friendlier than some.

The so-called French restaurant was fixed up like one of those sidewalk cafés in Paris, France. So, seeing the Indian summer weather they'd been having was still treating Kansas decent, Longarm allowed he'd have his supper seated under the awning out front.

He forgave them for appearing to brag when the waitress wearing an apron over her peasant skirts served him a right tolerable version of *pot-au-feu*, as you said beef stew in French. Their *vin ordinaire* was a pretty fair version of dago red wine, too.

So all seemed right with his world as Longarm dined alone in the gloaming, watching a pair of steamboats race one another downstream a hell of a lot faster than his *Creole Dancer* had ever taken him the other way when, out of nowhere, a voice dripping with venom demanded, "Deputy Long! What in blue blazes are you doing this far east? I thought I'd seen the last of you when I transferred here from Utah Territory!"

Longarm smiled up at what had to be the most chickenshit if not the most stupid field grade officer in the U.S. Army to say, "Well, howdy, Colonel Walthers. Set down and have some of this *vin ordinaire* whilst I tell you all about it?"

The lieutenat colonel who'd just never liked him stared wolfishly down at the carafe on Longarm's table to chortle, "You ordered table wine? You dared? In the dry state of Kansas? You're under arrest you insubordinate pup!"

Longarm easily replied, "Aw, hang a wreath on your nose. The brain inside just died. Neither one of us are state lawmen and if we were I'd like to see you try."

As he'd hoped, Walthers ran off down the waterfront, bleating for the local law like a triumphant sheep.

The exchange had not been lost on the waitress by the door. As the chickenshit ran out of sight she was shouting in French to somebody inside. A gent wearing an apron tore out the door, shouting back in the same. As he grabbed the carafe and Longarm's wineglass Longarm said, "Your way ain't going to work. We'd best try her my way."

The French chef sobbed, *"Merde alors!* Nobody has been so *précieux* about *vin du table* up to now! Is he some *species de farceur?"*

To which Longarm could only reply, "He's sure enough *something.* So here's what we'd better do."

71

Chapter 9

When the pompous officer came back with two civilians wearing copper badges they found Longarm enjoying his ice cream dessert with both the incriminating cruet and half-filled wineglass before him. The short colonel chortled, "There he is, like I told you, arrogantly holding himself above the law! Be careful! He's got a gun!"

One of the Kansas lawmen smiled warily down at Longarm to say, "I'm sorry, mister. Anyone can see you're new in these parts. But the law is the law and Kansas has gone dry."

Longarm nodded agreeably to reply, "So I hear tell. I'm the law my ownself. Federal. So suppose you tell me what state laws I might have broken."

The copper badge pointed at the evidence in plain view to demand, "Ain't that red wine we see on the table before you, and ain't red wine considered liquor?"

Longarm easily answered, "Well sure it is. But before this gets too silly to abide why don't you have a sip from this here carafe? I was using the glass to sprinkle it more delicate on my chef's salad, earlier."

The bemused Kansas lawman gingerly picked up the

73

carafe, sniffed it, scowled at it, and took just a sip before he sputtered, "Great day in the morning this stuff in *vinegar*! Who ever heard of red vinegar?"

Longarm patiently replied, "Can't you see this is a fancy French place? Ain't you never heard of fancy French vinegar? Ain't you got no couth in Kansas?"

The Kansas lawman so addressed indignantly replied, "Well of course we're couth in Kanas! What's this all about, stranger? This soldier blue says you told him it was red wine when you offered him some just now!"

Longarm chuckled fondly and suggested, "Get him to tell you about the time I knocked him on his ass out west. Me and Colonel Walthers go back to a jurisdictional dispute in the South Pass country a while back. Don't know why he can't get it through his thick head that I don't have to take orders from even *big* tin soldiers. But as I hope you can plainly see at this moment, he seems to be a sore loser who can't take a joke."

The two local lawmen exchanged weary glances. The one who'd been doing the talking said, "If I had the jurisdiction I'd run you both in. But seeing I don't, will you two lover boys work out your tiff and stay the hell out of our faces?"

He strode away, not looking back, nor did his sidekick, when Walthers bleated, "Come back here! Can't you see he switched cruets on us?"

Longarm swallowed some ice cream before he declared to nobody in particular, "Soon as I finish my dessert and settle my table I mean to cloud up and rain all over any short colonels in sight."

So the next time he glanced up he seemed to be dining alone again.

The waitress came back, smiling adoringly, to say his meal was on the house.

Longarm shook his head and replied, "That never would have happened had I not given that fool officer a hard time.

More than once. So seeing I got you all into the fix you don't owe me nothing for getting you out of it and I'm allowed six bits a day for grub on my expense account."

He'd have meant what he'd said if the place had looked more prosperous. Fair was fair and it had been his fight.

But they wouldn't let him leave without trying what she described as a *demi tasse au courant*, which was French for Irish coffee with the whiskey replaced by four-star cognac.

As she served it the waitress confided she got off by midnight. But Longarm turned in early, alone for a change, with the *Illustrated Police Gazette* and *Army Times* to give his love muscles a rest. For he had a busy day ahead of him and it was just as well they hadn't sent him to work with the Provost Marshal rather than the Remount Service. He'd have been in a fix if they'd wanted him to investigate missing cavalry troopers instead of cavalry mounts. Albeit had Colonel Walthers been charged with guarding the riding stock over at the Remount Station there'd have been less mystery.

The *Police Gazette* had more to say about those famous gangs of New York than horse thieves out west. The *Army Times* was concerned about the low rate of enlistments or reenlistments that might or might not reflect the Indian scares they'd been having border to border of late. Had Longarm been in the habit of writing letters to editors he'd have been tempted to write one, pointing out the Army hadn't raised a private's base pay since the war, whilst a top hand could make forty and found working cows that hardly ever scalped anybody, and a hard rock miner could bring home better than eighty a month with nothing worse than cave-ins to worry about and a woman waiting on him with a warm meal every time he came off shift.

A dirty little trade secret of the Indian Fighting Army as the Indian Wars wore on was the ever greater proportion of foreign-born or colored recruits it had fighting Indians, with the colored recruit having the edge as a soldier because he joined up speaking English and was used to hard work for low pay.

That "Thirteen dollars a month and all you can eat!" was a lie. The base pay was ten dollars a month with a three dollar a month uniform allowance tacked on. The trooper seldom got to spend that extra three dollars on anything but the outfit he was required to pass Saturday Inspection in. Officers paid the full cost of their uniforms, food and lodging. Enlisted men got their first uniform issued free but that was it for as long as they might serve. They didn't have to pay rent for a barracks cot or a patch of grass under a field tent. But they paid for any and all trail gear damaged or lost and as for all they could eat, they got what the mess sergeant served out and there were seldom seconds. So all in all, it seemed small wonder the Army was having a time recruiting any riders qualified to herd sheep.

But seeing it was none of his beeswax, Longarm got a good nights' shut-eye and when a steamboat whistle woke him in the morning he felt raring to go. So he got going.

He broke fast at another waterfont beanery and, leaving his saddle and saddle gun be, walked inland some distance to the sprawling military reserve with the fall weather holding sunny and dry.

For practical considerations of size and function, Fort Leavenworth was an open post, where they didn't stop you at the gate unless you had paint and a war bonnet on. But they had the usual sentries posted by the gate if only to give directions. So Longarm showed them the courtesy of flashing his badge and I.D. as he asked which way their Remount Station might be. When they pointed him along the right gravel path framed by whitewashed rocks he saw other civilians as well as more soldiers than one could shake a stick at, headed every which way on errands of their own. When Napoleon had allowed an army marches on it's stomach he meant it sucked up everything from ammunition to horseshoe nails like some bodacious rooting hog, and paid the going prices as it rooted.

Following the path past a drill field, Longarm saw a lance corporal whose apparent qualifications were a grasp of the English language giving a hard time to a gaggle of bewildered recruits as he bellowed in a mighty mean tone, "Hup, thoop, threep four. Pick it hup, thoop, threep four, with shoulders back, eyes off the ground, get your dress and cover down, if you 'spect a pass to town!"

Longarm muttered, "Keep that hup and someday they'll promote you to Lieutenant Colonel, you chickenshit!"

Unlike some veterens, Longarm seldom felt nostalgic about times such assholes had been allowed to yell like that at bigger boys. He knew an army had to have discipline. He wasn't as certain as to why it seemed the farther back from any *fighting* a soldier was, the more they got to act tough with him. The noncoms he'd followed through the gunsmoke of many a battlefield back east had just told him what to do next, without trying to sound like a barking seal.

Rank having its privileges, Longarm found an amiable staff sergeant in charge when he got to the Remount section. He said his name was Price when Longarm joined him by a training paddock, where a spunky young standardbred was circling the trooper holding his long lead in the center of the dusty tanbark. Longarm didn't ask why. The Remount Service was less inclined to saddle break a colt Texas style. They had the time and manpower to "Gentle" a mount to saddle and bridle. Broncs that had been "Busted" at five dollars a head by peelers of various skills were less predictable as their training advanced from accepting a rider to holding their position in a column of two or forming up for a stirrup to stirrup charge. The ways of a cowhand or cavalry trooper were neither better nor worse. They were just different. A heap different. Nobody was expecting a cowhand to cut an Indian out of the herd and rope him for branding. Nobody was expecting a cavalry trooper to fire a volley and charge a trail herd with drawn saber. It was said and Longarm had no call to argue, it was better to start with green kids and unbroken mounts the cavalry could train to do things their way. For there always seemed three ways to do most anything. The right way, the wrong way and the Army way. So horses and riders who've already learned other right ways could cause a heap of confusion in action.

Having learned some of both styles of riding, Longarm didn't waste time asking the fool questions reporters were forever asking about the Army way. Longarm knew the Remount Service bought and trained nothing but geldings because both mares in heat and studs anxious to serve the same caused trouble to more experienced riders, and so much for heroic cavalry officers leading charges on snorting spirited stallions. If that famous stallion Alexander the Great had charged around on had really been a stallion Alexander had been an asshole. And Robert E. Lee's Traveler had been a gelding, too.

Sergeant Price said they'd been expecting Longarm by name, adding how Colonel Walthers had been by earlier to give them direct orders not to cooperate with him.

When Longarm asked how Remount interpeted orders from Provost the sun-baked Sergeant Price said, "We have taken the matter under advisement. Some of the boys say you once kicked the shit out of Walthers. I sure hope that's true."

Longarm modestly confessed, "I only knocked him on his ass one time. He didn't have the sand in his craw for a fight. Don't you just love a cuss who won't fight you like a man and won't stop picking at you like a spiteful schoolgal?"

Price sighed and said, "Sure seems to be a lot of that going 'round in this man's army. We read that report from the town law at Jubilee Junction. Four of the nine horses in question may have been stolen from us. Hard to say since only that one white mount was recovered. We're not missing such a horse of a different color. I make it a mixed lot of stolen stock being herded cross country by those four who stopped at that smithy to have five more than we're missing reshod. Damned if I see why. Nobody tries to track government issue horseshoes on public rights of way. That would be an exercise in futilty. Every Army mount wears about the same mass-produced pattern and have you any idea how many Army mounts are on the move this fall, thanks to Sitting Bull and Victorio between 'em?"

Longarm nodded but said, "That wasn't it. They knew the stock they were herding had been reported stolen. They knew nine sets of fresh Army shoes in a bunch might raise an eyebrow or two. So, knowing how many sold-off Army bays there are along the highways and byways of this land, they thought they'd feel more comfortable herding Army bays looking to have been out a spell, traipsing about on civilian shoes."

"You're good," Sergeant Price decided, adding, "I never would have thought of that, even though you've just convinced me I should have! Where do you suppose they stole those other mounts?"

Longarm said, "Somewheres else, of course. Tell me something, Sarge. How long did it take you to notice them four you reported were missing?"

The Remount sergeant hesitated before he asked, "Long arm, do you have the least notion how many horses there are on this post?"

Longarm said, "That ain't what I asked."

Price said, "Counting reserve stock every regiment in this man's Army requires nine hundred mounts and we have training, reserve and headquarter troops here at Fort Leavenworth. That's in addition to the constant flow of new stock being saddle broke and . . ."

"You don't know, right?" Longarm cut in, not unkindly.

79

Price started to bluster, decided he might be among friends and said, "They were missing last Saturday for certain. We had a general inspection and unlike the usual Saturday inspection . . ."

"It was held for the commanding general," Longarm cut in. "Meaning everything and everybody was inspected more than once before the general made his rounds, with every button in place and every tent peg ever issued present and accounted for. Did the general himself notice your missing stock?"

Price morosely replied, "We told him we seemed to be missing four of our recently saddle broken replacement mounts. He was very big about it. Asked if we'd reported it and when we fudged a mite he let us slide under the wire and you've no doubt read the all points we put out. If our missing stock was part of that suspicious bunch reshod at Jubilee Junction we know they were last seen headed west. If they were another bunch of stolen horses our stock is headed somewhere else. Do you think it's one big gang, like some say?"

Longarm said, "I sure hope so. It'll be a bitch if this turned out to be a *fad*! Indications are we're dealing not so much with one gang of horse thieves as one fencing operation unloading them the same way with the same faked paper."

Price asked, "How come? I mean wouldn't it make your job tougher if they were to razzle dazzle with all sort of phoney bills of sale?"

Longarm answered, "They call it *provenance*. The difference betwixt taking a chance on going to jail by fencing stolen goods and walking free with a superior smile."

Putting on an indignant tone, Longarm recited, "How was I to know the horse, the grandfather clock or the Grecian vase I bought was hot, your honor? I know I got whatever at a bargain. But here's my bill of sale from the one who sold it to me and here's the bill of sale from the one *he* says he bought it from and here's this bill of sale from the Remount Service on a standard government form and how was *I* supposed to know it was an infernal forgery?"

As he saw that was sinking in he added, "That's how we know one mastermind's behind this rash of thefts. But it's also how he's been unloading hot horseflesh at a pretty tidy profit. The buyers can see the stock for sale is less than seven years old. They likely suspect it's stolen. But the solid provenance allows them to snatch up a real buy, feeling safe from the usual consequences, see?"

The Remount sergeant nodded and replied, "If you say so. But have you considered how that jasper you arrested in Denver *had* forged government bills of sale and he still got arrested, and then somebody murdered him?"

To which Longarm could only honestly reply, "I had not. But you're right. I should have!"

"Blow your whole notion into a cocked hat. Don't it?" asked Staff Sergeant Price, not unkindly.

Chapter 10

That unbroken mount in the training paddock was still going round in circles, too, as they were joined by an imperious figure in a black English riding habit, complete with veiled derby, seated side saddle on a chestnut standarbred of say sixteen hands. Her pinned-up hair matched the hide of her horse and she sat a horse well as she reined in to say she was looking for Staff Sergeant Price.

Both Price and Longarm doffed their hats as the Remount sergeant said she'd found him.

She smiled down like they worked for her, albeit she was a good sport about it, as she declared herself, "Godiva Hampshire of Sweetbriar Stud across the river," and added his major at the officers' club had told her to tell him they were at her service.

Price put his hat back on, replying, "You'll get no argument from this child about that, Miss Godiva. In what way may I be of service to you?"

She said, "I've been given to understand some stolen standardbreds were reshod the other night not far from here and that one of them was snow white. It so happens I am missing more than one white standardbred. We raise show horses at Sweetbriar."

Longarm was still holding his pancaked Stetson as he told her he'd seen such a critter the day before, adding, "Handsome gelding. Sixteen hands and sunny-natured. Might your missing stock be branded U.S., Miss Godiva?"

She sniffed, "Of course not. The Army can't meet the prices we set at Sweetbriar. We're talking about *show* horses, Mister . . . ?"

"Long. Deputy U.S. Marshal Custis Long, ma'am," Longarm replied, adding, "White gelding I got to pet over in Jubilee Junction was showy enough, I reckon. But he was Army branded and he'd been Army shod when the horse thieves left him behind."

Godiva Hampshite sighed and said, "Oh, pooh, I seem to be on a wild-goose chase, then. When I read about the mysterious doings in that dark-town west of the river I thought at least one of my poor dears might have been recovered. But, as I said, I don't breed Remount stock."

"Might I ask what tour show horses sell for, ma'am?" asked Price.

She answered, "Five hundred, minimum," with what seemed a clear conscience.

Price dryly remarked, "You're right, Miss Godiva. We've been authorized to bid high as two-fifty for an outstanding mount, thanks to the current Indian scare. But five hundred seems a little steep, no offense."

She smiled down sweetly to say, "None taken. We breed *show stock* at Sweetbriar."

Longarm asked, "Might you ever sell such fancy mounts to *officers*, Miss Godiva?"

She said, "Rarely. Not recently. Why do you ask?"

He shrugged and said, "My boss calls it the process of eliminating. It hardly matters, seeing the white horses you're missing were never sold and branded, and seeing no officers around here seem to be missing a white parade horse."

She said, "I should think not. Nobody below the rank of Brigadier is about to purchase a white charger if he ever expects to make Major General. Some senior officers can be jealous and spiteful as schoolgirls and my late husband told me that was what got General Custer busted back down to short colonel after the war. He would ride flashy in uniforms of his own design, like an officer of independent means."

When she got no argument about that she conceded, "*Band* officers are allowed to gussy up and ride *grays*, the same as other musicians. But we don't raise grays at Sweetbriar. Have any been stolen from other studs?"

Longarm nodded and said, "It 'peers so, Miss Godiva. We're still workin' on where some of them could have been stolen. We *thought* we had some gray mounts from Camp Weld a few days ago. But nobody has reported any white horses missing."

She said, "But you said that white horse those thieves left with that colored smith had been branded and shod by the Remount Service."

Price objected, "Not by *this* Remount Service at Fort Leavenworth, Miss Godiva. Maybe off some senior officer home on leave or . . . Ain't that something?"

She said, "I'm going to ride on to this Jubilee Junction. Could either of you say how far I have to ride?"

Longarm said, "All day, riding hard, cutting cross country, Miss Godiva. We rode forty miles or more east by rail and up the river about twenty. But, like I said, bee-lining from here might be less than fifty miles."

She glanced up at the morning sun and decided, "I'd best get cracking, then," and spun her chestnut round to light out at a lope.

The experienced Remount man said, "She's showing off. That's one handsome gelding. But it ain't about to lope no fifty miles."

Longarm nodded and decided, "She'll likely overnight at some wayside inn along the way. It ain't as if she can't afford it."

Price said, "I noticed the genuine pigskin saddle. Why do you 'spect she's riding so far after wild geese?"

Longarm shrugged and said, "Process of eliminating. I could be full of shit. She wants to see for herself. You have to kind of admire a gal with such a scientific approach to things."

"Any chance that *could* have been her missing white gelding?" asked the Remount man, adding, "What if somebody stole an unbranded and civilian shod horse from some stud, then branded it and shod it with Army issue to throw pursuit off?"

Longarm laughed and said, "I admire your devious mind, Sarge. But that won't work. In the unlikely event horse thieves with the skills to shoe stolen horses themselves felt the need to make a deal with that smith in Jubilee Junction, how long does it usually take a fresh brand to heal over and grow new hair?"

Price said, "You're right. She's on a wild-goose chase. We were talking about why they felt they had to murder that horse trader over in Denver if he had foolproof providence."

Longarm said, "Provinence, not providence. The one and original Jefferson Boyd likely would have walked, had he had the grit to hang tight and show those doctored government forms. We were trying to scare him into talking. Somebody was afraid he might talk. That meant he knew who the mastermind mind was. Most buyers wouldn't. Most buyers would buy from a middleman such as Jefferson Boyd. When we ran in Jefferson Boyd the wholesaler Boyd got those Army mounts off of must have shit and . . . Hold on! There's more! When we arrested him the one and original Jefferson Boyd seemed sincerely shocked he was offering grays for sale a few days after grays were stolen just outside the Denver city limits. The mastermind wasn't afraid Boyd would crack. He was afraid Boyd would come after him on a broom once we had to let him go. I know it ain't so and the mastermind knows it ain't so, but there's supposed to be honor among thieves and a Denver-based horse trader had every right to feel he'd had an umbrella shoved up his ass and opened wide!"

Price nodded and said, "I'd have been sore if I was running with a gang and they did me dirty as that. But how come any crook with a lick of sense would have done a pal so dirty?"

Longarm said, "Let's eat this apple a bite at a time. Mastermind could have been sore at old Jeff . . . that don't work. You don't set up a gang member to be arrested when you're afraid he'll give you away to the law. That leaves a desperate need for quick cash. Mastermind with gambling debts that wouldn't wait might take a chance on nobody noticing how close that ready money stock matched stock they never should have offered that close to home and so . . . You know what I'm doing, Sarge? I'm building a house of cards way in the middle of the air. If you want your house of cards to stand up you have to start from a firm foundation and I just ain't eliminated enough to stand shit on!"

The Remount man, dealing in horseflesh more than law enforcement, said he thought Longarm was building a swell house of cards. For he'd never considered half the angles they'd just been jawing about. He turned to call out to the trooper exercising the new mount, "That's enough for now, Jenkins. You got him sweaty enough. He ought to be willing to let you rub him down with that burlap smelling of human sweat. But mind you don't spook him so's we have to start all over!"

Turning back to Longarm, Price said, "Good help's so hard to find these days. Like I was saying, you've figured a gang grown big for its britches and taking chances for fast money as it struggles with the overhead of its own expansion and . . ."

"And you're worse than me at blowing bubbles in thin air!" laughed Longarm, adding, "We'd better quit 'fore we implicate President Hayes and Miss Lemonade Lucy. No telling who you might implicate once you get to complexicated conspiracies. For ain't it a well-known fact that Secretary Stanton engineered the assassination of Honest Abe and didn't you ever hear Queen Victoria was really a man?"

Price laughed and said, "I always thought it was Queen Elizabeth who was really born a boy. They put a dress on her so's King Henry wouldn't know. They didn't want him to know because he'd just cut off her mother's head and a boy child, being in line for the throne . . ."

"I'd best be on my way," Longarm cut in, holding out his right hand.

They shook and parted friendly. Had Longarm been on friendly terms with that short colonel over to the Provost Marshal's he might have had more questions to ask about their interior guard setup at Fort Leavenworth.

Seeing Colonel Walthers was more likely to give him a bum steer than a lick of help, Longarm decided to fall back on his own experience in such matters, putting two and two together from what Price had told him about a general inspection.

Interior guard, or keeping an eye on things during off duty hours was rotated through the ranks, with each trooper pulling it in turn as his name came up, averaging the duty every few weeks unless he was on his first sergeant's shit list.

Had it been up to Longarm, nobody would ever pull interior guard as punishment but it wasn't up to him and so he knew how many fuck-ups wound up guarding ammunition, valuable supplies and such they should have had guarded by their best men. So starting with a piss-poor to lackluster kid pretending to obey his first general order whilst reading *Captain Billy's Whizz Bang* in a latreen, any horse thief moving slinky under cover of night . . .

"Hold it! Back up!" Longarm warned himself, "Where in the U.S. Constitution does it say you have to steal Army mounts late at night? How would you sneak even one horse off the post late at night? Unlike the rotated *interior* guard, the MP company charged with *perimeter* guard *around* any post this size posts guards who've found a home in the Army and want to hang on to it!"

Trudging back toward the gate he mused, "No MP lifer who values his scalp wants a transfer to, say, Fort Apache at times like these. So you need a good story to get a horse by him late at night and even if he buys it he's sure to *remember* it! So how do we steal horses off a well-guarded military reservation without leaving a lasting impression?"

As he trudged on to the gate and passed through it without being asked one word by the two MPs posted there, a column of twos overtook him to go off on some training mission or whatever. The nearest MP saluted the officer at the head of the column but never challenged him.

Longarm nodded to himself and said, "Well, sure, those four Walter Lewis dealt with in Jubilee Junction, or somebody they were working with, rode through the gate in Army blue, rode on over to the Remount Station around the time the bugles were fixing to blow 'Retreat' for the day and cut out the stock they meant to steal in broad-ass daylight amid the confusion as everyone was knocking off for the day! How many buck-ass privates are likely to challenge, or remember, anything with stripes on its sleeves as it leads a horse to water or the Big Rock Candy Mountains? Didn't Price just say there was more riding stock on this post than you could shake a stick at and, hell, how often do you hear them holding a roll call for *horses*?"

Leaving Fort Leavenworth in his wake as he headed back to town to wire a dismal progress report, Longarm risked constructing, "That's likely the way they did her at Camp Weld. Like I just told the Sarge, you can get in trouble picturing things you never saw. Nobody raided Camp

Weld in the dead of night. These boys are too slick. Like burglars who break in at nine in the morning, knowing you've left for work, these birds just count on us picturing what happened all wrong!"

Walking closer to the river where things were more interesting, with the steamboats loading or unloading, the view across to Missouri being cut into individual Currier and Ives prints framed by landing sheds, piles of bulk cargo, grain elevators and such, Longarm wasn't paying as much attention to the landward side of the quay until a familiar she-male voice hailed him as *"M'sieur vin ordinaire!"*

He turned with a smile to see that French waitress waving her apron from out front of that shack they called a French restaurant. He hadn't meant to dine there again, not wanting to go through awkward comments about saving them a fine. But seeing it would have been even worse to openly snub her, Longarm ambled over to tick his hat at her, aiming to excuse himself and get it on down the river.

But she asked, "Did those friends who were searching for you find you, *M'sieu*?"

He said, "My friends call me Custis. I didn't know I had any here by the Big Muddy. Might they have said who they were, or what they wanted of me?"

She shook her head, sort of cute. Her head was round. Her eyes were big. Her mouth looked bee-stung and she had these spit curls he admired as she replied, *"Mais non.* But when I told them I knew neither your name nor where you were staying they asked if you might be dining with us again this . . . how you say *soir*?"

He replied, "Evening, I reckon. What did you tell 'em?"

She said, "I said I hoped so. They said they'd be back to see if they might catch you then. They left no messages *pour vous*. Nor did they say how they might be called."

Longarm asked what they'd looked like.

She told him they had struck her as *garcons du vache* which likely translated as cowboys. She said one was about

90

his age and the other a tad older. Both had been lean. Neither had been as tall as him. She recalled the older one as having had a mustache. A gray mustache more walrus-like than his. When he asked how they'd crushed the crowns of their hats she just looked blank. He didn't press it. There were green *cowhands* who didn't know it was traditional for riders north of the Arkansas River to telescope their Stetsons down out of the winds of the north plains, whilst most to the south cooled their scalps by having more air under a high crown.

He decided he'd worry about the way they crushed their crowns when he saw them. The question before the house was how he meant to see *them* before they saw *him*.

Chapter 11

Longarm knew the first rule of such situations was to take cover until you knew what the situation might be. Wandering the streets of a strange town with strangers you couldn't identify on sight holding the initiative could take fifty years of more off your life.

If that waitress was right they didn't know where in town he was staying. So that was where he blue-streaked to hole up and study on his other options.

The hotel being neither fancy nor a hovel it provided room service. Longarm bet the bellhop there was no way he could get up to the roof without the whole world knowing about it. After he'd lost that bet he ordered a pitcher of ice right off, with his dinner to be brought up around one P.M. Once things settled down upstairs he got a pair of field glasses out of his saddlebags and carried them up to the flat roof by way of the service stairs the bellhop had shown him.

He was a good quarter mile from that French place to the north but as he hoped, shaded by the hotel water tower, he could make the scene out clearly with the powerful field glasses and, better yet, nobody up that way was likely to make much of him against a distant skyline with naked eyes.

He couldn't look into the ambitious shed from his vantage point, but the angle would allow him to make out anybody seated out front and he had the time for looking about worked out. So he went back down to make himself a highball with washstand water, a hotel tumbler and the snake medicine from the same saddlebags, over plenty of that ice.

So after that it only felt like a million years as he spent most of the rest of the day holed up.

He went easy on the smokes and snake medicine, tried to make his dinner last, and went over all the reports he'd carried along in his saddlebags to read over when he had the time.

The mysterious strangers had surely given him plenty of time. So he got to read them all thrice without any pattern emerging, even though he had all his brass tacks hammered tidy in his mind as he stretched out on the bedding to rest his bones.

It hardly seemed fair. But nature wouldn't allow you to store up sleep the way you could store up fat and he'd already had a good night's sleep. But he forced himself to rest to the point of tedious, knowing he might have a long night ahead and hoping muscles kept in a stall all day might respond like a cooped up pony loose at last.

He tried not to leap to conclusions, discovering this was easy as sitting on a stump in the woods and not thinking about a big Russian bear. Had the strangers asking for him been sent from the home office they'd have known where he'd be staying. Had they known his name they'd have mentioned it to that waitress.

Since they hadn't, he figured they'd have no hopes of tracking him down by canvasing all the hotels and boardinghouses in town. Had they had that in mind they'd have had no call to lay in wait for him up at that half-ass sidewalk café.

"Somebody spotted us there last night," he decided. "Somebody without gumption to try it alone. Or mayhaps put off by old Walthers and those other lawmen so . . . that don't work. It was lack of gumption. He'd have hung about and moved in once Walthers and those others left. So let's say he bravely crawfished to another hidey-hole and sent those other jaspers to do . . . whatever he wanted done."

He reached for a cheroot as he decided, "That works. They got there too late to come back empty-handed for further instructions. The bird who knows me on sight if not by name had them try later, after I'd have been out of sight and out of mind a safe spell. So now they're hoping to join me for supper and won't that be fun?"

He knew if he went to the local law they'd back him up as he challenged the jaspers. But the local law already had him down as a cuss who made enemies of field grade officers and he could just see how things might go if the strangers simply held tight and allowed they'd read of the famous Longarm in the *Illustrated Police Gazette* and only wanted his autograph. Unless they were famous outlaws in their own right they only had to pay for their fancy French meal and nobody could do beans about them. You had to get a crook to make a crooked move before you could run him in. And wouldn't it be a bitch if it turned out neither was a crook? It was a free country and all sorts of pests from newspaper reporters to newsboys out to sell subscriptions had the right to see if they could set up a meeting with you at a place you were known to frequent.

It wasn't easy. But Longarm made himself sit still, comfortable as a cat on a hot tin roof, until it was going on early suppertime.

Once it was, he went back up to the roof with his field glasses to climb on up to the platform of the hotel water tower and have a seat with his back to the shady north of the massive tank with his elbows braced on his knees and the eyepieces up to his face, with everything a distant dark blur against the sunny southern sky.

He lit another smoke. He didn't have to stare constantly through the field glasses as long as he had a tight look from time to time. And time still passed slower than a snail race until, as ever in such cases, time suddenly commenced to race.

For two strangers dressed cow, both packing six-guns and one with a Big Fifty buffalo rifle, were out front of that French joint, jawing with that French waitress. As Longarm watched from afar the round-headed little thing was staring his way as if expecting him for supper. He had to tell himself there was no way any of them could see him in deep shade at such range. They both wore their hats north plains style. Longarm was not sure which was older or might have a walrus mustache. One or the other had a seat at the table out front. The other walked across the riverside way to circle a barn-sized pile of steamboat cordwood waiting to be picked up by some steamboat for its boilers. The cuss circled bold as brass, as if he belonged there with that buffalo rifle, mayhaps as watchman. He knew his onions. Nobody paid much mind to a man moving about in broad-ass daylight as long as he never moved *sneaky*. You always saw gents doing some fool something off to one side as you went about your own beeswax.

Longarm lost sight of that one for a spell as he spent some time out of sight on the river side of the cordwood, as if he'd gone to take a leak or enjoy a nap or write a book until nobody was likely to care.

Then, as was only possible from his higher vantage point, Longarm saw the sneaky son of a bitch slither like a snake over the far edge of the big woodpile and slowly sidewind his way across the split cordwood on his belly, with the buffalo gun cradled in his elbows. The Big Fifty was scope-sighted as well as overdeveloped. Its .50-170-700 cartridges were meant to drop a bull buffalo every time at 1000 yards. The range from the top of that woodpile to under the awning across the way was less than seventy-five.

"Those birds can't hardly want my autograph," Longarm decided as he made his way slowly down to the roof and strolled over to the stairwell shed as if he was raising pigeons.

Back in his room he drew his Winchester '73 from its saddle boot and quietly locked up to head down the back way with the same. His own rifle threw a .44 caliber ball weighing less and moving slower, but its popularity as a good enough man-dropper at 400 yards, with dead accuracy out to 200, fifteen times in a row, was well deserved. Longarm hardly ever shot at buffalo.

Having studied the lay of the informal street grid east of Fort Leavenworth from on high all afternoon, Longarm found it duck soup simple to work his way around behind that woodpile, unseen by the one across the way or the sneak atop it, and edge in to where, spying a ladder over against another pile, he was able to silently shift it, take a deep breath and ease on up it, knowing he was dead if the cuss topside was facing the river instead of that French joint to the southwest.

When he took another deep breath, got both feet up under him on a higher rung and straightened his legs to prop his elbows atop the cordwood, Longarm found his Winchester trained on the seat of the other man's jeans. So he levered a round in the chamber to add authority to his tone as he quietly but firmly declared, "Don't move a muscle and listen to me tight. I am not unkind by nature and I don't want to put a round right up your ass if I don't have to."

He had to. The desperado armed with all that buffalo gun chose to roll over and sit up as he swung the long barrel of his Big Fifty and this, of course, was a mighty stupid move.

As Longarm lay him flat on his back with a bullet in the chest the screaming cuss fired his Big Fifty wild and Longarm's reflex shot put a second round betwixt his spread legs to tear on up through his guts as far as it had a mind to.

Then Longarm was atop the woodpile, moving across the uncertain footing through his own gunsmoke as he levered more .44–40 into the chamber. When he got to where he could see down across the way the one who'd been seated under the awning was out in the road, pegging pistol shots up at him. So Longarm fired back and once more proved the old adage that a man who shoots it out with a pistol against a rifle at any range is almost dead certain to lose. Longarm dropped him easily and ran back to the ladder to descend post haste and circle the pile behind the smoking muzzle of his Winchester to see what he and Mister B. Tyler Henry, who'd really designed the Winchester, might have wrought.

Nobody was about to crowd a grown man with a smoking Winchester held at port, so Longarm and the other one he'd shot had a fair patch of trampled mud and horse shit all to themselves as Longarm stood over his man, pinning on his federal badge lest things get more confusing.

He could see, now, the older one with the gray walrus mustache had been wating for him under the awning, no doubt to lull him with some bullshit story whilst his younger pard atop the woodpile drew a bead on his back with those telescopic sights. The older one was still alive. Sort of. He stared thoughtfully up at Longarm to observe in a surprisingly conversational tone, "I think you spine shot me. Can't seem to move my arms or legs. Would you mind telling me your name, friend? I'd just as soon not die not knowing who killed me."

Longarm said, "I'd be Deputy U.S. Marshal Custis Long. You mean you and that other bird didn't *know*?"

The dying older man answered easily, "We were just doing as we were told. I warned him she'd have likely warned you about us. But ours not to reason why. Did you do old Chuck atop yon woodpile, bad as you done me?"

Longarm hunkered down to gingerly open the front of a bloody shirt with his free hand as he replied as casually, "Worse. Heart and gut shots. I fear you're right about your spine. Shooting from above like so I sort of got one down into your spine above your heart and below your Adam's apple. How bad does it hurt?"

The dying man replied, "It don't. I hardly feel nothing. I

ain't even sore at you for killing me. Ain't that a bitch? I know I *ought* to feel sore at you for killing me but all of a sudden it seems too much trouble and . . . Say, might you be the one they call Longarm?"

The man who'd just killed him nodded modestly and asked, "Would you mind telling me who *you* were, pard?"

The dying man said, "Oh, Lord, where do I start? I was named Knox, Knox Dewars, back in the days when I still believed all that bullshit in the Good Book. I'd like them to put Knox Dewars on my grave marker. Lots of the folk back home must be wondering what became of me."

Longarm asked if he had any more recent names. Dewars never answered. He was dead. They seldom lasted long, once they got to where they didn't care that they were dying.

Those same copper badges were edging forward from the curious but distant crowd. The one who'd sampled that vinegar the night before called out, "What was *that* one sore at you about?"

Longarm rose, Winchester aimed at the dirt betwixt them, as he called back, "Ain't certain. Ask the waitress, yonder, if they weren't laying for me, here."

The other copper badge asked, "They?"

Longarm waved the muzzle at the woodpile across the way to explain he'd shot another up yonder, adding, "Had to. He was out to do me with a scope-sighted Big Fifty."

The first one whistled and said, "You sure are popular, Uncle Sam!"

The other one agreed, "That's for sure. What makes you so popular?"

Longarm shrugged and said, "They both died without telling me. This one said his name was Knox Dewars. Sounds Scotch-Irish and he spoke with a Blue Ridge accent, so he likely was. Hat crushed north plains reads he came west direct after the war instead of by way of Texas. I know that feeling. He didn't know my name. It was purely business. Said they were working for somebody who knew me on sight."

The one who'd tasted that vinegar asked, "How about that short colonel who was after you last night?"

Longarm shook his head and said, "He knows my name. After that he's a chickenshit soldier, not a killer. If he was, he lacks the common sense to plan that far ahead. I find it curious any cuss who didn't know my name would send hired guns after me, though. Once I figure that out I might hazard who he might be. I hope your coroner will settle for my deposition. I was fixing to cross over to the Missouri side of yonder Big Muddy in the morning."

The two local lawmen exchanged looks. The one who did most of their talking said, "We may not know as much about French vinegar in these parts, Deputy. But we're up to date as any Paris, France, when it comes to formal proceedings. This ain't Dodge City or one of those other wild and wooly places Ned Buntline writes about! Nobody gets to shoot two men down like dogs, kiss the schoolmarm and ride off into the sunset! We got law and order around here. Dad blast it!"

Longarm nodded agreeably and asked, "So what do you reckon us lawmen ought to do next?"

The one who'd tasted the vinegar and still seemed sore about it told him, "You don't get to do nothing. This is our town and we are in charge of keeping the peace here. You let us see about carrying these old boys you shot over to the coroner's. Seeing it's getting late he likely won't want to convene an inquest until the sun comes up again."

Longarm said, "Damn it. I got places to go, tomorrow!"

The copper badge said, "Not before the coroner and district attorney says you can. You want to stay under your own recognizance within our city limits or would you rather spend the night as a guest of the city?"

Longarm said, "You've made your point. Is it all right if I go over yonder and have supper whilst I watch you boys tidy up?"

The one who didn't much like vinegar said, "You go on and do most anything you've a mind to. Just so's you don't leave town before they tell us they don't care."

Chapter 12

It reminded Longarm of a Leadville wine theater where you got to sup and watch a show at the same time. Like-minded citizens of the same bent, some of them courting couples out for an evening stroll, saw Longarm seated there under the awning and crowded in to grab a chair and order up. This gal at the next table giggled and said she'd never when her swain allowed they served French food there. The bitty round-headed waitress confided they'd never done such business before and said the cook inside had joked about asking *M'sieue Vin Ordinaire* to shoot someone out front every evening at suppertime.

Longarm laughed harder when she said the cook was kin but neither her father nor her husband. But after that he was stuck with the sad fact she was likely to be called as a witness by the county coroner and he had no call to compromise her.

That was what lawyers called a witness who'd been screwing gents she was speaking up for, a compromised witness, and, what the hell, she was only really tempting when she shook those spit curls.

Spit curls were supposed to lay flat, like they'd been glued to one's cheek with spit. The way hers went their own way when she swung her round head hinted at independent thinking and her head wasn't the only thing round about her under that shiny black sateen and white linen. Longarm suspected the perfume he smelled, mixed with her honest sweat, might have come from Paris, France, as well.

He allowed he'd try their *soupe a l'oignon* which he sampled up Canada way and cottoned to, followed by *chateaubriand*, which was close to beefsteak as Frogs ate. When she asked if he wanted his coffee with his grub in *la mode Americaine* he said he would and suggested Americans like to model their coffee in bigger cups than those demented tassles. So she said she'd tell them in the kitchen and that turned out right for her outfit, too.

As she later explained, they'd had to borrow regular coffee mugs off the regular American donut shop a few doors down. So as long as they had a bunch on hand she asked other customers if they'd care for their newest specialty, *Cafe á la mode Americaine* and everybody had said they liked it better. Their chef had declared he meant to buy bigger coffee cups and cash in on the fad. Longarm had the impression none of them had been out west long.

By the time he was considering dessert all the excitement out front had been cleared away and the riverfront traffic was getting back to normal as the streetlamps were lit against the gathering dark. A whole new local lawman, this one sporting a gilt star, came over to tell Longarm folk up and down the way, as well as the kitchen crew he'd talked to out back, sneaky, had all given much the same story about the earlier shoot-out and of course there was always the simple fact that the body atop the cordwood across the way had been that of a sinister young man with no visible means of support they'd questioned earlier about a horse left in his hotel stable.

"Stolen horse?" asked Longarm, motioning to the empty chair across his bitty table. But the local law said he had to be on his way, adding as he lit out, "We thought it might be. But he had a bill of sale for it."

Longarm rose to follow him, calling, "Hold on! You're just starting to give me a hard-on. Like I told you all earlier, I'm here on the trail of horse thieves! Tell me more about the cuss I shot atop yon woodpile!"

Not breaking stride as they both strode downstream, the lawman with the gilt star said, "Not a heap to tell. He was checked into the Fort Leavenworth Anchorage under the name of Will Johnson. Reckon he was tired of Smith or Jones and, like I just said, he'd left a suspicious mount in the hotel stable. One of them surplus cavalry nags sold off by Army Remount. One of our boys making his rounds got to wondering why any man who said he was a trail herder in from the Flint Hills and looking for work back the other way would ride a *cavalry* mount. You see, a high-stepping bay broke to charging or parading ain't the mount you want for herding cows. But he had a bill of sale and allowed his cowpony had gone lame on him so we figured . . ."

"I follow your drift. Fort Leavenworth Anchorage, you say? Might I find such a horse in its stable this evening, do you reckon?"

The local law frowned and said, "Hadn't thought of that. Reckon we ought to do something about that poor bay, seeing you just made it an orphan. But it's in its stall with fodder and water. So I reckon it's as handy yonder as anywheres else, overnight."

Longarm thanked him and peeled off, seeing the cuss was so anxious to get back to his checker game or whatever and seeing nobody was likely to raise the topic of search warrants as long as he didn't.

Longarm went back to the French joint to find a young couple seated at his table. The French waitress headed him off to sort of sob, "*Mon Dieu!* I did not know you were still *ici* and thanks to yourself we are so crowded *ce soir!*"

He soothed, "I was about done, ma'am. Came back to settle my tab and be on my way. What might I owe you?"

She asked if four bits sounded fair. He handed her a silver dollar and told her to keep the change as he ticked his hat brim to her and turned to go. But she tagged after, tugging on his sleeve as she repeated what she'd said before about getting off at midnight.

She shyly added, "I could ask to leave earlier, if you like. As a rule I stay on after we close around ten to help in the kitchen. But rules, they are made to be broken, *hein*?"

He sighed and explained there was a rule against defense witnesses who got off early for you.

She dimpled up at him to ask, "*Mais etre nous*, who is going to tell them?"

He laughed and said he might drop by later for some of their newfangled Americain coffee. It sure beat all how quick a man could learn enough French to get in trouble, considering how tough it was to *say* a damned word in it, right.

He knew better than to try such French Canuck as he knew on a gal out of Paris, France. Frogs were a caution for correcting a poor furriner who only wanted to know the way to the railroad station. As long as Americans, Dutchmen, Mexicans or even Paiutes had the least notion what you might be trying to say they were polite enough to go along with you. But even when they'd been born and reared American anybody who spoke French seemed to feel obliged to correct your pronounciation and give you a French lesson, the kind one gave with one's clothes on, instead of telling you where the infernal railroad station was.

He'd pointed out to no avail, to more than one pretty Frog, he felt no call to correct her English when she suggested something *très piquant* unless she produced some chains and whips.

It was fair dark in the stable behind that hotel down the way, but it only cost Longarm a dime to have a stable boy hold a lantern handy as he got to know that standardbred bay the late Will Johnson had left in their care. The Army brand on its near shoulder had long since healed. It was still wearing Army issue shoes. Its teeth described it as around four years old. Longarm had no call to examine the papers Johnson had shown the local law. No Remount officer worth his salt had ever sold off such a fine young gelding.

Getting into the dead man's hired digs upstairs was tougher. Longarm had to bet the night clerk more than a dollar he couldn't have a look around without a search warrant, seeing the cuss was never going to make it to officious checkout time, anyhow.

As Longarm had hoped he might, he found a McClellan Army saddle forked over the foot of the brass bedstead. The locals hadn't noticed that, or were too citified to wonder why a professional trail herder might be working cows with neither a saddle horn nor throw rope.

Professional cowmen seldom roped a beef critter, once it had been roped and branded that one time, if they could avoid it. Roping full-grown beef could bust bones or scar the hide. But on those occasions a man herding cows *did* want to rope one he generally wanted to rope it *serious*.

Opening the saddlebags behind the Army cantle Longarm hauled out the contents to toss them across the bedding. He smiled wolfishly and declared, "Jackpot!" when he spied the summer uniform of Army blue with a corporal's stripes and cavalry gold down the pant legs. The hat and boots Johnson had worn "On Duty" were over at the morgue with the rest of him.

Longarm found no other evidence as interesting. Most every rider had soap, spare socks and a dirty picture book in his saddlebags. Longarm put everything back the way he'd found it and let himself out. When the night clerk downstairs asked if he'd found anything Longarm said, "Nothing I wouldn't have expected."

The night clerk worked for the hotel, not the law, and he'd just now shown he could be bought.

Longarm thought about that, headed back upstream alone. The one whose horse and saddle he'd just tracked down had died without telling him a thing. But the other had said the two of them had been sent to kill him by a third party. If that third party was still in town he was afraid to try for Johnson's mount and belongings. Longarm knew that if he'd been in the rascal's place he'd have moved in fast, with the gunsmoke still hanging in the air up the way, lest somebody such as himself come by later to discover . . . what?

Longarm lit a cheroot and told it, "The two of them, along with most any handy others, rode out to the fort in broad daylight on their own bays, in uniform, to drive off those missing cavalry mounts along about 'Retreat' or mayhaps dinnertime in the middle of a busy day on a big busy post. Timing ain't as important as their methods and we'd best wire Henry so's he can put out an all points advising Army posts near and far to watch for strange faces in familiar uniforms, casually moving stock for no clearly evident reason!"

The cheroot, or that small voice in the back of his brain that was forever throwing water on his brighter notions, asked, "What if they up and change methods? Would you go on stealing horses the same way after two of your gang had been shot leaving all sorts of evidence behind?"

Longarm replied to himself, "You can only eat an apple a bite at a time. If they come up with another method they come up with another method. Just so we make the method they've *been* using too big a boo for them!"

He ambled over to the Western Union nigh a bigger steamboat landing and got off a detailed night letter to his home office. Night letter rates cost less for more words and nobody was going to do much with his message before the night letter was delivered in Denver in the morning.

Longarm considered taking what he'd just found out to the local law. He decided since he was going to have to repeat it all before a coroner they could wait on the little he had. But as he strode along he considered how much he had and decided it was better to be safe than sorry.

The odds on the one or more survivors pussyfooting over to that hotel to make off with that Army bay or the Army saddle up in Johnson's room were slim. Seeing what they might have to gain for all they had to lose. But few college professors took up a life out along the Owlhoot Trail and a lawman could never go wrong underestimating the intelligence of a crook.

So he asked directions, mosied to the town lockup and told the night man he'd have staked out the Fort Leavenworth Anchorage if it had been up to him. The night man said it wasn't up to him, but allowed it seemed a notion worth passing on when his superior came by, later that evening.

That left Longarm with a clear conscience and not quite as much time to kill. He drifted closer to the military reserve and killed it bellied up to the bar with off duty troopers, being a sport when it came his turn to buy a round and getting a better line on current gossip in the ranks.

He'd made certain he was drinking with regulars, since recruits had mighty odd notions of the Indian-Fighting Army. Regulars on duty a good distance from Mister Lo had odd enough notions about him and the best ways to cope with him. Longarm never corrected the know-it-all who pontificated about Sioux never attacking at night and Apache *always* attacking at night. The rules for fighting Indians seemed more clear as they were recited farther away from Indians. It seemed a crying shame the ignorant savages didn't seem to know the rules. But Longarm was more interested in current desertion rates.

They were always high. For many a young buck who'd thought it a swell notion to get tattooed or join the Army on

107

a Saturday night had sober later thoughts and it was easier to back out of a three-year hitch than "Death Before Dishonor" or "Forever Mother Dearest" needled into your hide.

Your average just-plain-dumb kid deserter was usually brought back in no time by the MPs, wondering how in the world they'd known where to search for him as he dug latrine pits or made little rocks out of big ones. He was usually cured of running home to Mother Dearest after some kindly Prison Chaser explained how the Army had your home address on file.

After that there were the professional deserters or bounty jumpers, who gave a fake name and home address as they joined up to collect the cash advance extended to new recruits and then simply faded away like the old soldiers they never were. The late Will Johnson had likely come by that uniform that way. There was no way to tell. Bounty jumping was a petty but almost perfect crime. There'd been talk of photographing new recruits and the British had been experimenting with fingerprinting the Hindu laborers who signed up to build a road and ran off with tools and dynamite. But the jury was still out on how practical, or certain, such identification might be. So, meanwhile, the U.S. Army, like all the other armies, leaked men, materiel and livestock in a manner to get everybody in Washington fired if the taxpayers ever learned the true numbers. Longarm had read in a book by a Mr. Gibbons that the Roman legions had wasted money even worse. Such numbers seemed to go with having armies, it would seem. But they'd only sent him out in the field to see if he could cut down on the loss of riding stock.

He knew Billy Vail would have never approved. But Billy was in Denver as Longarm allowed he could go for some of their newfangled American coffee and one of those Crappy Susans as he sat down at that same table along about ten.

The same waitress allowed they'd commenced to clean up out back and a flaming *crepe Suzette* would require not only some time but the use of a substance forbidden under current Kansas law.

He said he'd forgot you made a Crappy Susan with burning brandy and asked if she had any other suggestions.

She said, "*Mais oui!* I have given thought to what you said about our becoming how you say compromised? I think we must leave *tout de suite* and continue this . . . *conversation seur la rose, non?*"

Up Canada way they'd told him *seur la rose* meant under the rosebush, but when they got there it was this bitty houseboat tied up in a backwater down a ways. She said her name was Simone and nobody else would ever know they were there, or what they might have been doing there.

Chapter 13

Simone said she'd rented the houseboat and fixed it up with the chinz curtains, velveteen cushions and such, all smelling of hard scrubbing under *potpourri*, which was a mighty strange French notion when you studied on it. *Potpourri* translated literally as "Rotten Pot" but smelled like a mishmash of flower petals and spices, which was what it really was. You could smell things better than you could see 'em because Simone relied on the rays of a streetlamp on the quay a few yards off, shining down through the bitty windows on that side. Her place might have passed for a frilly little bedchamber in some fancy house if it didn't get to rocking every time a train of waves from a passing barge or passenger boat sloshed her backwater.

There were times for talking and times for action and when an unexpected pitch of the carpeted deck staggered Simone against him Longarm took her in his arms for some action.

He knew he'd been right about how unbalanced she'd really been when they somehow wound up staggering over to her bed, and damned if they didn't wind up falling across it.

She said those passing steamboats were a caution. He

agreed with her. Sort of. His exact words were lost with their lips together so friendly.

As he shucked her out of her pongee and linen he saw he'd been right about how rounded everything under it kept working out. Simone was a more compact brunetted version of the blond Miss Bubbles back in Denver, the stenographer gal named for the way she filled her courthouse costume.

But for all her round curves and French manners, Simone welcomed him like a long established lover with her warm and natural charms. So he responded in kind, mounting her as if they'd been shacked up a spell and their bodies had gotten to responding in three-quarter time, with each knowing which way to thrust and twist. Things went that way, every hundred years or so, and it really felt grand to be home again.

The time for talking came, as ever, once they'd come, more than once, and settled back to share a smoke and some pillow talk.

Longarm was too polite to say most men didn't care to hear how good girls had gone bad. So, seeing confession felt so good to the she-male soul, he had to sound interested as she went on about losing her cherry and her reputation at the age of sixteen during that Franco-Prussian War, making her later in her twenties that night. The dashing French *chasseur* who'd promised to do right by her once he'd won the war had never come back from the war. She confessed that for the sake of her good name she hoped he'd fallen as a hero. In any case, the resulting village gossip had sent her off to Paris, cussing right back at them and so what with one thing and the other she'd wound up serving *chasseurs Americaines* as long as it was understood she served them nothing but *haute cuisine*. And so she'd been getting lonely, *mais a huis clos* with civilians who understood the needs of a woman of the world . . .

Male or she-male lovers who thought you needed to know all about their previous fornications sometimes blew up on you if you bragged on your own slap and tickle. So Longarm never went into the gals he might have loved and left, marching off to his own war. Hoping Simone wouldn't slip up at the coroner's inquest he coached her some in such plain English as she could manage. That naturally steered their pillow talk to the case he was working on. Simone was worse than no help at all. She made dumb suggestions, based on some mighty odd notions of Indians, the Indian-Fighting Army and the horses they both rode.

She'd been reading French translations of Ned Buntline and that Herr May who wrote western whoppers in High Dutch about Noble Savages. Savages got more noble as they got farther away. The term had been coined by that Mon Sewer Rousseau who thought French peasants just wanted to play patty-cake, too, and managed to die just in time to miss that French Revolution.

When Simone suggested the mysterious white horse left with the blacksmith at Jubilee Junction might be an officer's trophy horse, captured off the Indian, he explained, "Indians ride big white geldings, or any horse they can get. But most so-called Indian ponies are scrub stock, a lot of it captured wild. Wild scrubs tend to breed scrubby. Sometimes to the point of dwarfish. Professor Darwin calls it reverting to type. We humans have bred critters we want to ride bigger and faster than nature. Them runty Shetland ponies, descended from Norse stock Vikings abandoned on their way home aboard crowded longships, stand closer to the natural stature of a natural horse. A horse Indian band on the move don't look so romantic in the flesh as in a painting. Albeit the warriors do ride the better mounts and some nations, such as the Cayuse and Palous, have taken to selective breeding with fair results. Most Indians mounted on a noble steed stole or swapped for it. Stealing a horse is considered a deed to brag about by most every Indian nation. The famous Lakota chief, Shunka Wakan Wasichu, got his proud handle from stealing a heap of cavalry mounts. His name is usually translated as 'American Horses.' They'd have ridden up Canada way with more cavalry mounts than usual after Little Big Horn but by now most of 'em would be due to sell off if Remount had its say."

She'd read about Custer, in French, and objected only one noble cavalry steed had survived the battle and was he not the mascot of his regiment at the moment?

He patted her sweet rump and chuckled, "You're talking about the famous Comanche, Captain Keogh's personal mount. They found him there alone, shot up bad, and ran up some veterinary bills to keep him, as you said, as the mascot of the 7th Cav. Many a stablemate had been shot up worse and then the Indians had rounded up the ones they could use. They had no use for a critter who appeared fatally wounded, of course. None of the horses they captured that day were snow white chargers, or even gray band mounts."

She said, "Simone, she think when you find out who the horses of another color were stolen from, the mystery, she will be solved, *hein*?"

He kissed the part on her dark hair and said she was likely right. That inspired her to see if she could get it up for them again with her bee-stung kips, and damned if she couldn't.

It was just as well they got along so well. For to Longarm's growing dismay he was stuck there three whole days, with the nights easier to bear on Simone's houseboat.

The coroner gave no sensible reason. He was just one of those petty-fogging political hacks out to milk all the newsprint he could with the fall elections just around the corner. By the time he held his hearing reporters from the *Kansas City Star* were in the hearing room.

They were likely as disgusted as Longarm by the time the coroner's jury had decided a federal lawman was only acting natural when he shot sinister unknowns out to assassinate him in front of scores of witnesses up and down the way.

Simone was only one of Longarm's local admirers who'd witnessed a pure and simple broad-ass daylight shoot-out. The one who'd described his fool self as Knox

114

Dewars had been aiming at Longarm when Longarm fired and nobody climbed atop a barn-sized woodpile with a scope-sighted Big Fifty to take a sunbath.

They hardly bothered with Simone's testimony, once they saw how tough it was to understand it. But Longarm assured her she'd done swell as they did it dog style back in her houseboat after the hearing.

He figured he owed her that much before he crossed over into Missouri. She was a good sport about it, or mayhaps commencing to wonder, as so many lovers did by the fourth night, if that was all there was to love and life.

Next morning a ferryboat took Longarm and his baggage across the Big Muddy to Platte County, Missouri, named for yet another Platte River that joined the Big Muddy downstream from its more serious namesake. Platte just meant "Flat" and there was a lot of that going around in those parts.

There being no livery service at the bitty landing, Longarm bought a mule off a farmer for ten dollars and saddled it up to be on his way to the Sweetbriar Stud Farm. They told him he had less than a morning's ride ahead. The mule didn't see things that way. They argued about it 'til they were coming up on a roadside stand where some raggedy farm kids were trying to sell produce. They stared thunderghasted at the first customer they'd ever had when Longarm reined in and dismounted to ask if they had any carrots.

The big sister of ten in charge said they sure did for a penny a bunch and Longarm bought ten bunches. He'd tried selling produce at a roadside stand when he was little. The delighted child threw in a slightly used paper bag.

Longarm let the mule have a sniff before he lashed all those carrots but one to his saddle swells. Then he asked the same kids if they could sell him a big stick.

A little brother allowed he'd noticed some windfall under a nearby mockernut tree and Longarm lit a cheroot to wait as the kid ran to fetch him a stout branch. Longarm asked if they'd take a nickel for it and with that transaction out of the way he got out his pocketknife to trim the fallen branch into a sort of Irish shillelagh as the kids and his tethered mule watched with interest.

"Aw, don't club it, mister!" gasped the kind-natured young gal as Longarm advanced on the mule with a carrot in one hand and that stick held high in the other.

Pausing before the mule as it tugged back in vain on its securely tethered reins, Longarm told it in a conversational tone, "You're old enough as well as stubborn enough to know what a fed-up rider can do to you with this stick. Let's see if you're smart enough to make a deal with."

To the delight of the kids and the surprise of the mule he fed it the carrot. As it chomped away on what tasted better than the sugar cubes some spoiled equids with Longarm said, "They say mules are more stubborn than horses because they have better memories. So I'll thank you to just remember there are more carrots where this one came from and now I want you to carry me to Sweetbriar with no further nonsense."

It worked. The mule trotted along in the crisp morning weather as if it really wanted to go somewhere and Longarm kept his word by feeding it another carrot when they broke trail once an hour along the way. So well before noon, directed the last stretch by some colored kids with a goat cart, Longarm rode through the imposing gateway of a spread surrounded by a whitewashed rail fence.

The sprawl of whitewashed housing for man and beast ahead must have set their owner back a piece in whitewash alone. As he'd hoped back in Kansas, Godiva Hampshire of the chestnut hair and expensive riding habits had beat him back from Kansas with time to spare and there she stood on her front veranda with a riding crop in her hand, an angry look on her handsome face, and an armed and dangerous-looking Missouri rider standing to either side to back her play.

But Godiva smiled friendly enough when she recognised Longarm as the law. She called out, "Get off that freak of nature and let us put your saddle on a serious horse. You're just in time for some serious cross-country riding. Soon as Uncle Nero gets here with his serious coon hounds. The sons of bitches drove off through tanglewood where the only trailing is by scent!"

As Longarm dismounted a colored groom took the mule's reins to lead it around to the back. Longarm joined Godiva and her white hands on her veranda, asking about that white gelding in Jubilee Junction.

She said, "Barking up the wrong tree. It was a good old boy and you were right about it being friendly. But it wasn't the white charger I lost."

She stomped her booted foot like she just hated her veranda and told him, "Whilst I was riding back we lost *another* prize show horse. This one jet black, save for matching white stockings and a diamond blaze. We figure it was stolen in the dead of night, along with two bay saddle brutes I was asking four hundred apiece for! Nobody heard them sneaking in or out. We only knew the stock was missing at dawn, when our stable boy went to water them and didn't find them in their stalls."

Longarm whistled and asked, "Prime stock, stolen from your stable instead of roaming loose in pen or paddock?"

One of her hands asked, "Weren't you listening, famous lawman? Didn't you hear what the boss lady just now said?"

Longarm smiled thinly and, using the same tone of voice he'd used earlier on that mule, he replied, "I listen swell. Sometimes I ask the same fool questions and listen some more. They call it conducting an investigation. So let's investigate that chip on your shoulder, friend."

Godiva said, "That's enough. I've enough on my plate this morning and yonder comes Uncle Nero!"

Longarm turned to see an older but spry-walking colored man coming in with a half dozen redbone hounds. He wasn't holding them by leashes. He had those dogs trained. They never broke ranks even when a yellow yard dog came around a corner to yap like a coyote pup throwing a temper tantrum. It broke off and ran for its life when Godiva snapped at it.

Longarm asked, "You have yard dogs roaming at large, Miss Godiva?"

She nodded and said, "I know what you're thinking. The thieves most likely spoke gentle and tossed some treats ahead of them as they moved in slow. One of the stable boys found a cube of pork liver out back as we were scouring for sign."

As Uncle Nero and his more serious hounds came within conversational range, Godiva called out to ask if the messenger she'd sent had filled him in on her most recent losses. Longarm noticed she spoke to the older man respectfully, as if he really was her uncle.

Uncle Nero addressed her as if talking to a queen, replying, "Yass'm Miss Godiva! I came as fast as these old legs could get me here! Me and my hounds is at your service, Miss Godiva."

She nodded and said, "Let's all go around to the stable yard, then. You'll be riding with us, Uncle Nero. You do know how to ride, I hope?"

The elderly colored man who'd doubtless started out as property said, "I knows how to ride, Miss Godiva. I just ain't *used* to it much."

As he led his hounds around the corner of the big house the white hand called Seth grumbled, "You're putting that coon on one of our *horses*, Miss Godiva?"

She answered without batting an eye, "You're talking about *my* horses, Seth, and I want to trail the ones we're missing fast as Uncle Nero's hounds can track, not fast as Uncle Nero can *walk*. So let's get cracking."

Longarm liked her even better when she added in a softer tone, "Local custom be damned. It's not *right* to ask a man that old to track on *foot* whilst the rest of us ride!"

Chapter 14

Where they weren't yet under cultivation the bottom lands along both sides of the Big Muddy were timbered with leaf-shedding hardwoods such as alder, cottonwood, box elder, plain elder, elm, sycamore and so on where the woods hadn't been recently logged off. Where they had the stumps were woven together with sweetbriar, blackberry, and other brambles with most every vine but poison ivy armed with thorns.

So Uncle Nero's hounds had their work cut out for them as they picked up the scent and followed it, baying some, through the shin deep fallen leaves. The purloined stock had been led due east, then northeast to due north as far as a logging path through the bare-branched timber. At which point the hounds commenced to circle and whimper more than they bayed, with some of them rubbing their muzzles in the forest duff.

Uncle Nero dismounted to join his redbones on his hands and knees as he sniffed at the leaf-covered trail himself. He sneezed and got back to his feet to call, "Black pepper, Miss Godiva. Can't say how far and wide because black pepper don't stand out in the leaves the way red pepper might. The gents who stole your stock have stolen stock before!"

The surly Seth at her side said, "I'll bet they headed for them swamps along the Platte. Do they lead them any distance in fetlock-deep swamp water, having the lead on us they must, our only hope is somebody they've passed recalling old White Socks."

She turned in her sidesaddle to ask, "What do you think, Deputy Long?"

Longarm said, "I think Uncle Nero knows these woods and his own hounds better than this child. I vote we let *him* decide."

Seth muttered something under his breath. Longarm was good at reading lips but let it go. He was forever getting himself called Indian lover, Jew lover, Chinee lover or some sort of lover by know-it-alls like Seth. It saved a know-it-all thinking for his own self when he knew anybody who didn't think he knew it all had to be party to dark plots.

When Godiva Hampshire asked Uncle Nero which way he figured they'd gone the old tracker honestly replied, "I don't know, Miss Godiva. But I 'spect I knows how we might pick up the trail again."

She told him to do as he thought best. Not meeting Longarm's eye but nodding at him in passing, the old-timer led his hounds back a ways on horseback and then proceeded to circle through the woods about a furlong out from the peppered patch.

"What does that fool nigra think he's doing?" growsed Seth as his sidekick they called Lenny had the brains to set his horse and watch. Godiva caught on right away. She said, "No matter where they went with my stock from where they peppered their tracks, they'll have left sign for Uncle Nero to cut farther out! Did *you* know he was fixing to do that, Deputy Long?"

Longarm shook his head as a silent white lie. Folk who

120

bred horses likely knew less about tracking them than folk who stole them and had he said the old colored gent's ruse was standard tracking procedure old Seth might have felt even dumber, and know-it-alls made to feel dumb were inclined to do dumb things about the same.

Seth got to feel better when the distant hounds commenced to bay again and Uncle Nero pointed to the northwest. Seth chortled, "I *told* you all they was headed for them swamps! What have you got to say about it now, Deputy Long?"

Longarm replied, "When you're right you're right," in a cheerful tone. It would have been rude to add the Good Book allowed wisdom often came from the mouth of a child. The message being it was smart to listen to everybody because the laws of averages allowed most anybody to be right *some* of the time.

So they chased after Uncle Nero an hour or more until things got confusing some more. You called a nigh impassible stretch of mud and quicksand a bog. You called flooded meadows a marsh. You called a nasty tangle of flooded forestlands a swamp and they sure had some along their smaller Platte River.

Like many other such chains of open water and flooded stickerbrush, the swamp called the Platte River ran in line with the wider channel of the Big Muddy for miles before joining up with it. The reason was sort of sneaky until you talked to geology professors. It seemed that all over the world, wherever big muddy rivers ran, they built natural levees along their banks by spilling mud over them at high water. So smaller streams running into the big ones got turned aside by the natural, often wooded, levees to mope and poke along beside the main channel, searching for an opening and piling up their own muddy confusions.

The reasons for the soggy mess were less important than the results. The hounds commenced to howl more like coyotes with toothaches as they splashed like kids in the water. It was Lenny's turn to say, "Such current as there may be in that stagnant water has had plenty of time to carry the scent of three horses most anywhere."

Godiva said, "More than three horses. The thieves must be riding others. Which way do we go, Uncle Nero?"

As the white folk set their mounts the old tracker and his hounds circled clear around them, only getting wetter. Seth said, "They only got to follow the swampwater, upstream or down, for as many miles as they care to and it's already past dinnertime!"

Then Uncle Nero let out a whoop from way the hell upstream and as they splashed close enough to make out his words he said his hounds had picked up the scent again.

They bayed off to the west, which was toward the Big Muddy in that neck of the woods because of the way it meandered all over Robin Hood's barn on its way to the Mississippi nigh Saint Lou, far to the east. As they followed Uncle Nero to slightly higher ground nigh the main stream—it only had to be a little higher—the footing got drier but the woods if anything got thicker until they busted into logged-out cottonwood above the landing Longarm had made earlier. Godiva was first to recognize a distant form tethered to a stump near the water's edge. She cried out, "White Socks! It's him! He's safe! He must have busted free!"

Longarm let Seth tell her, "He's tethered in place by the lead of his rope halter, Miss Godiva!"

She didn't seem to care as she loped on to where the black gelding seemed to have been expecting her. White Socks pricked up his ears and nickered as he pawed at the fallen leaves with a hoof.

As the rest of them caught up she'd dismounted to circle her handsome show horse, patting it and examining it for injuries. As they joined her she looked up to marvel, "Not a scratch on him! Sound as a dollar and he couldn't have broken away! What could this mean?"

Longarm kept his opinions to himself. Seth opined they'd ferried the other stock across to the Kansas side, abandoning the show horse because it was a show horse, who'd be remembered everywhere they led the others.

Godiva asked Longarm directly. He shrugged and said, "Makes sense to me. Eight hundred on the hoof, inconspicuous, seems safer to fence than a show horse one can recognize at a quarter mile."

She said, "I thought we'd agreed they'd been stealing horses of another color."

Longarm shrugged and said, "They might have noticed we'd noticed. Or we might be talking about two sets of thieves. You have to keep an open mind about such matters, Miss Godiva. One reason your Frank and Jesse are still at large is that blaming them for every train robbery across the land has lead to mighty confusing notions as to their whereabouts."

She said, "Whatever. The point is that I have my White Socks back and I aim to keep him." She nodded at Seth and added, "You and Lenny had best carry him home to Sweetbriar whilst Deputy Long, Uncle Nero and me ride on in search of the others."

Seth objected, "That don't sound safe to me, Miss Godiva. I know they say the famous Longarm can whup his weight in wildcats and I'm sure Uncle Nero is ferocious as his hounds. But we've no way of knowing how big a gang we're after!"

Godiva patted the stock of her Ballard saddle gun and allowed she could take care of herself.

Seth looked as surprised when Longarm said, "Seth's right, Miss Godiva. The bunch played games with another show horse at Jubilee Junction was tallied as a quartet. There's nothing in the U.S. Constitution saying we might not be tracking more than that. You and White Socks will be safer if we all stick together, no matter where we go from here."

She untethered the black show horse and handed its lead up to Lenny as she asked Longarm, "Do you think they escaped to Kansas with my other stock or could they have had something else in mind?"

He waved his free hand out across the muddy water as he decided. "If I aimed to ferry stock across a river I'd have had a flatboat or at least a raft waiting here. I don't see where any vessel of any description has been run up in yonder muddy shallows. Don't see any hoof marks or even human footprints crossing all that open mud, neither."

For the first time since they'd met, Seth grinned at Longarm to say, "By gum he's on the money, Miss Godiva! Listen to the man! Maybe he deserves to be famous!"

She soberly asked, "Uncle Nero?"

The old tracker said, "I sees how they slickered us, now that they's slickered us, Miss Godiva. They went on up old swampwater with the other stock whilst jes' one of 'em led White Socks out where the hounds could track him. After he tethered us a false lead he backtracked along the same scent trail to chase after or jes' go on home. Hounds ain't been trackin' *his* mount."

Godiva nodded and asked, "Why are we standing here? We know which way they must have gone. Let's go on after them!"

So they did, or tried to. They cut back to the swamp to slosh north as the hounds tried in vain to cut sign to either side. The wooded swamp got narrower and trended ever more wide of the Big Muddy as it came in at an angle from the north. The lush growth to either side spelled out how rich the bottomland was under all that unimproved tanglewood. Longarm could already see a future where the Platte would run as a narrower and tidier stream through cultivated farmlands. But in the meanwhile it was a soggy bitch, even as it narrowed, and they had a far piece to slosh before they ran out of swamp entire.

It got worse where an east-west corduroy road had been

punched through at right angles. The hounds hesitated and circled uncertainly, sniffing at the trampled mix of sand and clay spread across half-buried logs as they tried to make up their minds. Uncle Nero explained, "All sorts of critters from other horses, mules or oxen use this trace, along with all sorts of wild critters such as deer, coons, rabbits, skunks who aim to cross dry. Do I push my hounds on befo' they sure I could push 'em clean off the trail. Do I waits for 'em to decide, we could be here a spell."

Godiva asked, "How far are we from Sweetbriar, now?"

He said, "Past sundown, Miss Godiva. Do we follow this wagon trace out of the swamp we still g'win be caught by nightfall on the trail."

She watched the hounds circling for a spell before she decided, "I have my White Socks back. Let's carry him home and lock him up tight! They have too good a lead on us with those poor bays and that'll learn me not to brand my stock!"

As they followed the corduroy road east Longarm didn't ask why a stud operation didn't brand the colts it had for sale. The Army was only one among many who preferred its own brand on the stock it bought. But when she asked he said he'd wire Army Remount but doubted it might do much good. He said, "Trying to sell a black gelding with matched white stockings and a diamond blaze is one thing. Offering bay standardbreds with most any forged bill of sale during a national emergency is another. They'll get caught if they try to unload your stock at Fort Leavenworth. So they likely won't try. The one big operation I'm out to break up has sold stock all over to *civilians* as surplus army stock and even if we could reach all prospective civilian horse traders by wire, how many are about to overlook a literal real steal? Them forged government bills of sale attached to less-convincing paper makes it easier for them to unload obviously stolen stock, even as it makes my job of backtracking easier."

She objected, "I thought you said these birds who stole my White Socks don't have to be the same bunch."

He sighed and said, "They don't. They acted sensible about a horse of another color. But my boss calls what I'm doing a process of eliminating. I can't say whether your stock was raided by one bunch or the other 'til I do some 'liminating."

"Are you allowed to arrest them if they're not part of the gang they sent you after, Deputy Long?"

He said, "My friends call me Custis and as a paid-up peace officer I can arrest anybody, anytime, for beating any law. Getting a conviction in a federal court if I ran in a Kansas bootlegger might be complexicated and if I catch local talent stealing Missouri stock I'll turn him over to Missouri Law and let them handle the paperwork."

"Then you do mean to go on working on my case?" she asked.

He nodded and said, "Long as it's still warm, leastways. Wouldn't I look the fool if it turned out later you'd been hit by the very gang they sent me after? There's this tendency for lawmen to run 'round in circles like headless chickens, chasing leads great, small or imagined. I try to follow one lead at a time. You can fail that way often enough."

She asked what the odds on solving a particular case might be.

He grimaced and conceded, "National average is one in seven when the guilty party ain't on the scene when we get there. Most serious crimes are solved by somebody pointing a finger and yelling out who done it. Ain't as easy when nobody can say who done it."

She marveled, "One in seven! Dosen't that get discouraging . . . Custis?"

He said, "I do a little better than average. But you're right about it getting discouraging at times. I've been trying to establish a pattern for the mastermind I'm after. So far overconfidence is the only trait he, she or it has shown.

Any old pro who'd compared notes in prison would know better than to use the same government forms over and over again or deal in horses of another color."

She pointed out, "They abandoned that white show horse in Jubilee Junction and just now left my White Socks for us to recover. Might that not mean they're wising up about horses of another color?"

Longarm sighed and said, "I fear you could be right. If they stick to selling off bays, switching to other bills of sale, we may just be talking about fish that got away!"

"What do you do when fish get away, Custis?" she asked.

He replied, "What does anybody do when fish get away? You go home empty-handed, hoping you'll have better luck next time!"

Chapter 15

The corduroy road across the swamp soon gave way to a regular wagon trace, with Uncle Nero's hounds investigating more horse apples and cow pats than you could shake a stick at amid the wind-blown fallen leaves. As the going got drier the woods got patchworked with homesteads, many of them carved out of the oft-flooded bottomlands by free colored folk. They got coffeed and caked by some white truck farmers Godiva knew and it was just as well. None of them had eaten all day.

Godiva turned down their invite to stay for supper and spend the night there. They regretted her decision before sundown when it commenced to rain.

Longarm had his slicker lashed to his McClellan. None of the others did. Godiva protested it hardy seemed fair when he insisted she wear the only slicker there was. But he said he'd feel worse, dry, if he let her ride wet. So she accepted gracefully, allowing she was sorry she hadn't thought ahead.

He laughed and allowed few riders did, singing a few bars of the old trail song that went

Cloudy in the west.
Looks like rain.
And I left my slicker in the wagon again!

The words got dirty after that so he stopped. But the rain didn't and it was coming down fire and salt as night commenced to fall. It fell by just getting darker. It was too nasty out to watch the sun go down.

They loped their mounts ahead when they heard banjo music somewhere in the dowpour ahead. Godiva and her locals knew where they were going.

Longarm knew most anywhere was an improvement on being out in the rain. They galloped into the deserted barnyard of a rain-lashed homestead to see at a glance the banjo music and cheerful light from paper lanterns was spilling out from the gaping barn door.

As they reined in yard dogs came out to fuss at them but a big fat colored gal waved them in, she said, to her daughter's wedding.

Others risked getting drowned to help them with their riding stock. As the five of them joined the bigger bunch in the barn they could see at a glance the wedding party was colored, gussied up as best they could manage and sincerely friendly.

Longarm could tell, since they all seemed to know Godiva Hampshire, she had to be the sort of white neighbor described as "Quality" in darker circles. He'd thought she seemed all right.

Shucking the slicker to hand it back to Longarm, as if it was likely to do him a lick of good *now*, Godiva led the way to the refreshments atop one-inch planks across saw horses. They'd arrived too late for the demolished wedding cake but there were plenty of pork chops and hush puppies left, whilst the punch was real punch, laced with white lightning, because they weren't in Kansas anymore.

Godiva greeted a teenager trying to look like a cowboy as Raymond and introduced him to Longarm as one of the stable hands who'd been on duty, over to her place, the other night. Raymond said he was overjoyed to hear they had White Socks back. He said he was still working on how they'd gotten past him and some other kid called Wallace.

Longarm said he admired Raymond's outfit. The kid said he meant to be a cowboy out west when he finished growing up. His folks kept telling him he wasn't old enough to strike off on his own.

Longarm said his outfit was mighty convincing, just the same. Missouri was west of the Mississipi but they still raised more horses, mules and corn than beef cattle. Yet, just the same, Raymond had sprung for a boss Stetson, a red sateen shirt and Justin boots flashed with those sassy "Gal's Legs" spurs

Longarm never mentioned them, hoping Godiva might not catch on to the pornographic design. At first glance Gal's Legs spurs, made back east by a novelty outfit, looked like irregular spurs of mayhaps hammered brass. On second glance you saw the naked legs of a gal embracing the heel of the boot as if it was a bawdy house customer. The rowels of the Gal's Legs spurs were held more coyly betwixt the ankle of another pair of naked legs with bent knees. Longarm considered whether Raymond shuffled his feet so awkward because he knew what he wore on his boots. He sure felt awkward about something and he should have been used to working for a white boss who treated him right.

The newlyweds had gone off to get consummated shortly after serving out all that wedding cake. So the party was mostly hanging on because it was raining too hard for anyone to go home.

But everyone there was country, brought up to go to sleep with their chickens, so by nine even the banjo player was starting to nod off. The fat lady of the house, Godiva called her Mammy Jones, offered to let her white guests bed down in the house. When Godiva asked where that might leave her and her own, Mammy Jones explained they'd just carry their bedding to the hayloft up above.

Godiva shook her head as if used to getting her way and told the older woman she and the boys would bed down in the hayloft. So Mammy Jones told everyone else to go home 'cause Miss Godiva needed some rest.

In the confusion, nobody thought about bedding. Longarm had his bedroll handy. Neither Godiva, Seth, Lenny nor of course Uncle Nero had one bedroll between them.

Godiva put up the same fuss about Longarm's bedroll as she had his slicker, with the same results. She and her hands bedded down in the back of the hayloft. Uncle Nero and other colored orphans of the storm settled in near the front. You didn't really need bedding in a hayloft, if your duds were dry. But Longarm had been looking forward to shucking his wet duds and crawling bare-ass into dry bedding.

Sleep being out of the question for a spell, Longarm climbed down the ladder, mosied across the now dark dirt floor and lit a cheroot to lounge in the doorway as the rain seemed to be letting up.

Things were down to an occasional frog plop when he heard cautious footsteps and turned to howdy young Raymond. The kid who'd been headed for the door jumped half out of his skin to come down protesting, "I ain't done nothing, captain! I was only fixing to go on back to Sweetbriar, seeing the rain's let up."

Longarm broke out another cheroot as he said, "Keep me company a spell, Raymond. I want to talk to you about those horse thieves over to Sweetbriar the other night, when you were on night watch."

Raymond protested, "Along with Wallace, captain! I wasn't the only one and I ain't used to being 'cused of things!"

Longarm pressed the smoke on him and lit it from the tip of his own as he said, "I figured Wallace would be in on anything anybody was in on. But he never came to the wedding and you did, in a fancy outfit that must have set you back a bundle. Anybody can see Miss Godiva treats her help right, but neither Seth nor Lenny wear expensive Stetson hats, Justin boots or sassy Gal's Legs spurs. Stable boys must do better here in the Show Me state than back where I grew up in West-By-God-Virginia."

"I saved up," Raymond tried.

Longarm said, "Whatever. Let's talk about yard dogs. When I rode in to Sweetbriar, earlier, and this Jones spread tonight, I wasn't out to steal stock. I wasn't acting sneaky. Yet yard dogs barked at me both times. Ain't that a bitch?"

Raymond tried, "Me and Wallace was wondering about that. Found some pig liver on the stable floor and . . ."

"How?" Longarm cut in, adding, "Pig liver wet or dry hardly stands out from the trampled straw and horse shit on your average stable floor. Do you have white tile stable floors at Sweetbriar? Even bare gray cement? I fear the sworn testimony of them yard dogs would be enough to arrest you on, Raymond."

Raymond let the three-for-a-nickel smoke go to waste on the dirt floor as he sobbed, "Oh, Lordy! You can't 'rest me, captain!"

Longarm said, "Sure I can. I got a gun. But hear me out before you shit your jeans. I know they told you boys you'd never get caught, but you did and after we carry you both to the county jail the sheriff is fixing to put you in separate cells and offer you both the same deal. The sheriff is going to say the first one who talks is going to get off as a friend of the court, whilst the last one to talk is going to prison as a horse thief, if he's lucky. It'll be up to the sheriff to see nobody takes anybody out of his jail to hold a late night rope dance."

"We never stole Miss Godiva's stock, captain! I swear to Jesus on the water and I don't want no white boys coming to get me in the night!"

Longarm said, "Things don't have to be that way, Raymond. I know you stable boys just looked the other way after somebody crossed your palms with thirty pieces of

133

silver. But you ain't the ones I want. I want the ones who led you boys and them geldings astray."

So they fenced and bargained a spell as he'd figured they might, Longarm was writing names down in his field notes. A deal was a deal so he never withdrew any offers when it developed the horse thieves he'd wasted so much time on seemed local talent.

At least that solved the mystery of the horse of another color. He didn't need Raymond to tell him trash whites who meant to fence the stolen bays just up the Big Muddy at Saint Lou would have been out of their minds to hold on to the widely admired White Socks.

The sneaky Rayond sniffed, "You don't have to tell Miss Godiva, does you, captain? She always treated me and Wallace right and I don't see how we'd ever be able to face her if she knowed!"

Longarm said, "I won't have to tell her if I don't find either of you there when I return the rest of her stolen stock to her. So why don't you and Wallace head out west to be cowboys, buffalo hunters or whatever?"

Raymond said, "My folk say I's too young, captain."

Longarm said, "You weren't too young to aid and abet the theft of stock you were being paid to guard. You do as you've a mind to, Raymond. I'll do what I have to if I find either one of you two-faced little shits on Godiva Hampshire's payroll when I get back to Sweetbriar."

Raymond lit out on foot, sniffling with self-pity. Longarm muttered, "Let's hope I don't need that bedroll tomorrow night!" as he went to scout up his borrowed mount and personal saddle.

Uncle Nero caught up with him in the tack room. As Longarm unforked his McClellan from its saw horse Uncle Nero said, "Them boys be gone by the time you gets back to Sweetbriar, Deputy Long. I too old to be much help but I can rustle up some boys to back you' play if you likes."

Longarm didn't want to insult anybody. So he never

pointed out the fuss that might ensue in the Show Me state if a colored posse brought in white horse thieves. He said, "Since I'm federal and ain't got all year, I aim to recruit me some Platte County law before I move in. They'll be holed up, waiting for the search to cool down. So now that I know where they can be found, I mean to wrap things tidy with a cast iron local indictment and as little noise as possible."

Uncle Nero nodded soberly and asked, "Would you find it uppity if I was to offer you my hand, Deputy Long?"

Longarm replied soberly, "I'd take it as an honor, Uncle Nero."

So they shook with mutual respect and Uncle Nero helped him saddle and bridle the cordovan mount Godiva had loaned him.

He asked Uncle Nero to tell the lady he hadn't stolen another horse off her as they walked the cordovan outside. Uncle Nero was laughing as Longarm rode off through the night, making for the nearby county seat at where else but Platte City.

He got there before one A.M. and the sheriff's deputy at the night desk said he just didn't know.

Longarm said, "Sure you do. Lend me a fresh mount, back my play with a couple of riders and we'll all be famous in the morning! The horse thieves of which I speak are three in number and likely slugabed a little over an hour's ride from here. What do I have to do, get down on one knee and serenade you? Didn't you always want to be a lawman when you grew up?"

"Before I go rousting boys out of their own sluggy beds, can you prove them Fletcher brothers stole Miss Godiva's stock? They ain't never been charged with horse theft before."

Longarm said, "Let it be on my head if I'm wrong. It happens. Raymond could have sold me snake oil. On the other hand if they have her stock it's open and shut and, like I said, we'll all be famous!"

The night man said he'd see about it. He let a half-sober gent they'd been holding overnight out of the drunk tank and sent him to fetch Duke and The Kid. As the drunk left he waved Longarm to a bentwood chair and said, "Take a load off. May take a while."

Longarm asked about that fresh mount. The night man shook his head and said, "Ain't authorized. Have to wake up our county wrangler and he's a mean son of a bitch when you *don't* wake him up in the middle of the night!"

Longarm decided to let it go. Godiva had loaned him a good mount and as tough on the poor brute as it might go, stuck the whole night with one mount might save some back and forth riding, later, if things worked out.

How well things might work out was up for grabs. Sitting down and lighting up, Longarm asked the night man if it was true Frank and Jesse hailed from the next county over.

The Plate County Deputy nodded and said, "County of Clay, now that you meantion it. Why do you ask? You don't think Frank and Jesse had a thing to do with raiding Sweetbriar, do you?"

Longarm said, "Not hardly. It's just now come to me how Frank and Jesse could have remained at large for going on fifteen years with a known home address."

The Platte County lawman nodded knowingly and said, "We've jawed about that some. You'd think Clay County would put a tad more effort into it, seeing them boys rob the bank in the county seat so regular and everybody knows where they stay when they're home with their momma. Reckon the law over yonder ain't professionsome as us."

Longarm just smiled.

The deputy thought before he went on, "Might be *kin* to Frank and Jess. Ever'one in the County of Clay seems kin to ever'body else. They say the Younger brothers are kin to the James brothers and how about old Jesse marrying up with a niece named after his own mother? Don't it strike you as mighty Old Testament to marry one Zerelda when your momma's name's Zerelda?"

Longarm conceded, "Sounds as if it might confuse such reporters out our way as Ned Buntline. They've already confused our Jesse with Robin Hood."

Then the surly Phil and sleepy Duke stomped in, gummy-eyed but bearing arms. So Longarm forgot about the James and Younger boys as he led them off to arrest the Fletcher brothers.

Chapter 16

The county lawmen knew the way and as the brisk night riding woke him up the one called Phil recalled the two younger Fletcher boys lived under the thumb of an older brother and his play-pretty.

Phil said, "They describe her as Creole and say she's just a housekeeper but she's still a she-coon sharing the bed of Brother George. I think they call her Chrissie. Ain't that a bitch. She's fat as a pig and black as the ace of spades!"

"What about yard dogs?" asked Longarm.

Phil thought and answered, "Now that you mention it, I don't think they have none. I don't remember none, the times I've been by. Most places you stop by to deliver election flyers have dogs they got to call off you. But the Fletchers don't. I wonder how come."

Longarm said, "You just answered that, Phil. Dogs barking late at night are heard far off, and remembered by those they wake up. Folk running a stop along the Owlhoot Trail are likely to have strangers visiting them at all hours and they don't want the neighbors talking. Can either of you describe the innards of the Fletcher place to me?"

Duke said, "I can. I served a search warrant out yonder

one time when a neighbor 'cused Chrissie of helping herself to a brace of them red chickens as lay brown eggs."

"Rhode Island Reds?" asked Longarm.

Duke said, "Yeah, them too, and the original owners were sore as hell. But we never found no red feathers or brown eggshells and we were trying."

"We were talking about the layout," Longarm urged.

Duke said, "Two main buildings, aside from the shit house, chicken coops and such. The two younger brothers have separate rooms in the four room cottage. Other rooms are the kitchen and all-purpose, along one side. Big brother George and his so-called housekeeper have one end of the stable set up as a lovey-dovey, with the tack room betwixt them and the six stalls. They got a corral out back as well as a fenced-in meadow they let stock graze. Apple orchard on the far side of that, with a woodlot beyond. They grow no truck nor corn. They say breeding horses keeps 'em busy."

Phil said, "You know, now that I study on it, they don't keep no broodmares nor studs. They seem to raise geldings by immaculate conception. How come I never thought of that before?"

Longarm said, "Nobody asked you to."

He didn't have to tell them how often lawmen acted on their own when they'd heard no complaints. They were both lawmen.

It was after two and a moon shining fuzzy in a still moist sky shed just enough light for them to manage without bumping into things as they dismounted in a woodlot a furlong out from the Fletcher place to move in on foot with their saddle guns held at port.

All the windows stared back black from the whitewashed moonlit walls. The layout being as described, Longarm muttered, "Why don't you boys take the house whilst I bust in on the brother who sleeps alone?"

Phil said, "George don't sleep alone. They only *say* that she-coon is their housekeeper."

Longarm said, "Means we don't have to worry about where she might be. I doubt they'll have outside doors locked if they're in the habit of moving back and forth across the dooryard. Why don't you boys see how close you can get to the little brothers before you wake 'em up? I'll take Big Brother George. Seeing he's the one I'm most anxious to have a word with."

They didn't argue. It felt sort of spooky walking into a moonlit homestead with no dogs barking nor even a chicken clucking.

Trusting the county men to their own chores, Longarm edged on to the stable and tried the latch to discover the door wasn't locked. He eased it open. As he moved toward another door inside a horse in one of the stalls nickered. Longarm froze, the muzzle of his Winchester trained on the barely visible square of inside carpentry. The damned horse nickered again. The bedroom door flew open and two guns blazed as one.

The burly figure who'd fired a Dance Brothers' .45 from the doorway was only visible as a pair of bare feet with their heels hooked over the sill as the gunsmoke cleared. Longarm had no idea where the other man's pistol round had hit. It hadn't hit him. He was about to call out when a gal mostly visible as a white nightgown appeared in the doorway in a spooky way to drop to her knees by the head of the late George Fletcher whilst, somewhere in the night, two more shots rang out.

Longarm said, "I'm sorry about this, Miss Chrissie. But you heard him fire first."

What still looked like an empty nightgown worn by a haunt sobbed back at him, "My George meant you no harm. None of us mean no harm to nobody and . . . Oh Lordy, what's to become of me now?"

A distant voice called, "Longarm? You all right in there?"

Longarm called back, "I am. Old George ain't. The other two?"

The voice he now recognized as that of Duke called back, "They both resisted arrest. Don't see how we'll ever manage a trial, now. Ain't that a bitch?"

Longarm struck a match with his free hand and got the nearest wall sconce going to observe that in the lamplight, a very large and very dark woman had been wearing that white nightgown all the time. Her face was sort of child-like. He couldn't help feeling for her as she stared up at him like a kid with a busted arm to plead, "Where's I gonna go? Who will take me in? My George was the only white boy who ever 'spected me and now look what's happened!"

Longarm decided she was as comfortable where she was, with the dead horse thief's homely bewiskered face cradled in her big soft arms as he went on oozing in her lap. Lowering the muzzle of his Winchester Longarm made much the same deal with her as he'd made earlier with Raymond. When she heard she might not have to go to jail if she leveled with him she leveled with him.

After that they hadn't told a play-pretty who seemed a tolerable cook all that much about their horse trading.

Chrissie had heard mention of black, gray and white show horses as things to be avoided. Her George had been vexed with his kid brothers for stealing Godiva Hamp-shire's White Socks when they'd made the deal with those stable boys Longarm had guessed at. He'd said a horse that was tougher to sell wasn't worth the risk no matter what you might be able to ask for it. He'd said something earlier about the brains of some Collier boys over to Clay County, stealing that judge's mount. She couldn't tell Longarm when they'd decided to use White Socks as a red herring in that swamp and seemed to feel he deserved not to know af-ter shooting a poor boy who'd meant him no harm with that Dance Brothers' .45. He couldn't get her to tell him more about the Collier boys she didn't know or some judge in another county.

Longarm went out to join the others in the dooryard. He

suggested they notify the county coroner and let his crew tidy up out there. When Duke asked, "What about the gal?" Longarm said, "Leave her to heaven. She ain't but a molested child they were using as an unpaid servant and play-pretty. If Platte County plays its cards right she'll think she just escaped and nobody will have to do anything about her, the poor thing."

So that was about the way they worked things out, with Duke riding in to the county seat as Longarm strung Godiva's two bays on one long lead. They were easy to pick out from the others on hand. Anyone could see they were worth twice as much as a fair cavalry mount.

Phil thought he ought to stick around for the coroner. Longarm told him, "I'll be at Sweetbriar or they'll know where to find me. Like I told you coming out this way, I was never sent all this way to solve bush league cases such as this and if you play your cards right, you and Duke will get all the credit you deserve!"

Phil decided he had a point and they parted friendly with the mount he was riding dragging its hooves, but, what the hell, Sweetbriar wasn't all that far.

When they broke trail a few miles on the cordovan was hanging its head like it was fixing to founder. So Longarm changed his saddle to one of the stolen but less pathetic-looking bays, telling it, "I know you was run through woods and swamps the same as that big sissy, Brownie, but fair is fair and he has been ridden more this evening."

The rescued bay didn't argue. Longarm remounted and rode on, to trot the three of them in just before dawn, inspiring dogs to bark, roosters to crow and Godiva Hampshire to run out across the dooryard, barefoot, in her own white nightgown, praising the Lord.

Which hardly seemed fair to Longarm when he considered half the trouble he'd gone to on a false lead.

Longarm never commented when stable boys he hadn't met before came out to take charge of the riding stock and his saddle gear. As Godiva led him toward the big house, arm in arm, she said Raymond and Wallace had both quit. He nodded and replied, "Raymond did say something about heading west to herd cows."

They met Seth, Lenny and some other help on the veranda, nobody but Longarm fully dressed. Godiva told them all to go back to bed or get ready for breakfast.

She told her colored cook in passing she and her guest, Deputy Long, would be breaking fast up in her quarters. The cook didn't argue. Nobody seemed to argue with Godiva Hampshire.

Once she had him up in her bedchamber, sitting them both on her rumpled bedding, Godiva demanded he tell her all about the miracles he'd just wrought.

He was repressing some yawns as he went over it all again. He'd told the same story so many times and it had been a long night. It seemed as if he'd last been to bed, with Simone, back in days of yore.

But Godiva was a fast study and before he told her she saw those late Fletcher boys hadn't been tied in with the gang he was after.

He yawned and said, "I was hoping they might at least *know* something. We don't think the bigger operation consists of one big gang of horse thieves. It's more a rash of thefts inspired by a conspiracy of fences, offering young Army stock at over-the-hill prices with the help of the fake government paper I mentioned earlier. I'm still working on where they got those horses of a different color, or what it might mean. Few show horses have been reported stolen and even if many had, those trash white Fletcher boys knew better than to offer such stock in shady horse trading circles."

He yawned again as she suggested, "They left that one white charger with that blackmsith over in Kansas. Might that not mean something?"

He yawned again and asked, "What? Why have they been stealing such stock and above all *where* have they been stealing such stock? It makes no sense no matter which way you hold the page. Yet I somehow feel that if only I knew what them horses of a different color were doing in an otherwise straightforward fencing operation everything would fall into place."

Then he had to wonder where all that music was coming from as he and Godiva rode round and round on the merry-go-round with every horse a different color. There were pink horses, lavender horses, red, white and blue horses, with the one he was riding grass-green.

He hoped Godiva wouldn't notice he was riding her merry-go-round without a stitch of nothing on. The last time he'd found himself in such a fix it had been at a funeral, with him wishing he had at least his hat to cover his privates, even though none of the others filing by the flag-draped coffin seemed to have noticed at first.

This time, on the merry-go-round made up of horses of different colors he noticed he wasn't the only one bare-ass. Godiva was riding the sky blue mount ahead of him with nothing to cover her shame but her long chestnut hair and it was blowing out behind her. He wondered if he could see her tits if he spurred his grass-green mount up even with hers. He kicked at it with his bare heels and Godiva soothed, "Don't twist and turn so! You'll yank it out if you don't lay still!"

So he lay still long enough to see she seemed to be riding him instead of that sky blue pony and snorted, "Aw, hell, I'm just having a wet dream!"

But he wasn't, exactly, as he opened his eyes to hear the music stop and the light all different, staring up at Godiva in such morning light as slipped in through the slits of her window shutters. After that she was still on top of him, and he was still in her, as she moved up and down like a kid on a merry-go-round, looking mighty mature with those tiger stripes of morning light rippling up and down her athletic curves. It beat all how athletic rich gals could curve without enough fat on 'em to matter. Albeit Godiva curved way different than Penny Mansfield or mayhaps Westfield had.

The comparison inspired Longarm to roll Godiva on her back and finish passionate and she didn't mind at all, judging by the way she laughed and thrust her trim hips to match his efforts.

Neither had said anything about what they were up to until the two of them had shared a long shuddering orgasm. As they just floated there amid the pink clouds, Godiva sighed, "That was heavenly. You must think I'm an awful slut."

Longarm kissed her, putting some steam into it, before he told her, "I never call angels in heaven sluts, Miss Godiva. But I was sort of wondering how we might have got there."

She dimpled up at him to say, "It was your own fault. You fell asleep on me and after I'd dismissed the cook I tried to put you to bed for some well-earned rest. I used to do that for my husband when he fell asleep after working himself half to death. But as I pulled down your jeans you were . . . I think they say showing it hard and, seeing it had been so long, and seeing it seemed to be calling out to me, I guess I lost my head!"

He kissed her some more and said, "I'm sure glad you did. For I'd have never had the nerve to make a play for you in the time we had to work with."

She moved her hips experimentally as she asked if he meant to go some place soon.

He thrust back, replying, "I ain't certain how soon, but I got to ride on sooner or later, Miss Godiva. That Chrissie I told you about may have given me another lead. I got to ride on to Clay County and ask around about some judge who might be missing a white show horse."

"Do you think she could have meant that white Army horse they've impounded over in Kansas?"

He said, "Can't say before I ask. Horse of another color in Kansas wore Army shoes and an Army brand. On the other hand nobody's reported such a horse stolen, but some judge not too far away might have some answers."

She said, "Oh, damn! How soon do you have to ride on? Couldn't you at least . . . keep a girl company until tomorrow morn?"

He held her closer as he conceded, "Reckon I'd best stick around long enough to see if Platte County wants a deposition about them Fletcher brothers."

So she said she'd see he got a swell breakfast, as soon as he made her come some more.

Chapter 17

Longarm suspected it might be what rich folk called breeding when he noticed how, like the darker Penny Mansfield,
Westfield, Whateverfield, Godiva spared him the life story
so many woman seemed to feel they owed every man they
went to bed with. He suspected rich folk, like Army vets
who'd really seen action, were less inclined to talk about
themselves because they had more to brag on, had they
wanted to, but didn't want to. Everyone but born bullshit
artists knew nobody wanted to hear how great anyone else
might be.

After serving him grits and gravy for breakfast in bed,
Godiva said she'd feel better about their "relationship" if
they got dressed and went through the motions of tending
to business, saving the coming night to get related again.

So it was later in the day, during casual conversation
with the hand called Seth, he learned where Godiva had
learned to rape unconsious men.

Seth said her late husband had been older, drank some,
and he'd died in his prime of a heart stroke after his sawbones had warned him he was working and playing too
hard.

Godiva never mentioned her late husband again. He

wanted to ask her views on that other rich gal who seemed on the run from a husband. But he feared she might take his curious nature wrong. Rich folk were a caution when it came to such speculations. Another rich gal had once told him that the redheaded Princess of Wales greeted rich gals everybody knew her fat husband had slept with as if nothing had happened. They called it being sophisticated. He wondered what old Billy Vail's wife would do if she ever caught him in bed with Miss Bubbles from their stenographic pool down the hall.

By sundown they had everything running smooth again at the Sweetbriar Stud and Longarm forgot all about Penny as he pictured Miss Bubbles or bubbly Simone in bed with him and the longer limbed Godiva. The longer limbed Penny wouldn't have been as much fun, he felt sure, as he did old Godiva dog style with his eyes shut, picturing the same view of good ol' Simone. Godiva giggled and asked what had gotten into him. He never told her. He never told any of them, nor did he want to know who *they* might be picturing with his old organ grinder in *them*.

Next morning, after another filling breakfast and less argument from a gal who said she wasn't used to that much fornication in the course of a single night, Longarm was off for Clay County aboard that mule he'd bought in Platte County, having refused Godiva's offer of a real horse for Gawd's sake. He knew what they said about boys who'd accept an expensive gift off a gal they'd given themselves to.

The seat of Clay County was called Liberty. It was bigger than Platte City. That didn't make it all that big. It lay a little over twelve miles to the southeast of Godiva's spread. So they made it in a little over four hours, easy, with dinnertime winding down around Courthouse Square.

But when he asked at the sheriff's department about any local judge missing a white show horse they had no record of any judge filing a complaint on any missing horse. Longarm sighed and said, "Well, it was a nice ride and you got a pretty town here. But it must have been another judge in another town."

A younger deputy brewing coffee on the potbelly stove looked up with a thoughtful frown to ask the deputy Longarm had been talking to if that *general* hadn't said he was missing a white horse.

When the one in charge allowed that sounded right, it developed a newly arrived pain in the ass, a retired officer who seemed to think he could order civilians around, had filed a complaint on a lost, strayed or stolen personal mount, described as a white standardbred frisky four-year-old!

Longarm asked how to get to such a retired pain in the ass. The deputy he'd been talking to led him outside and spying a passing townsman, called him over. He introduced the sort of prissy young dandy to Longarm as their own Bob Ford and asked the kid, "Could you carry this lawman up to General Churchward's place, seeing it's on your way, Bob?"

Young Ford said, "Sure. It's just up the hill, Mister . . . ?"

The deputy who'd introduced him said, "Just said he was U.S. Deputy Long, Bob. You got wax in your ears?"

The kid smiled sheepishly and said, "Got my mind on other matters, family troubles. Come along with me, Deputy Long. Like I said, it's just up the hill."

Longarm tagged along on foot, leading the mule. When young Ford asked how come he'd been riding so droll, Longarm said, "Been riding to get there, not for show. Long story. Suffice to say I've been out to cut the trail of some horse thieves."

As they trod the brick walk up the hill Bob Ford said, "I have some kissing kin trading horse in Saint Joe. Used to like him better before he beat up a favorite uncle. Do you think that's any way for kissing kin to treat one another, Deputy Long?"

Longarm easily replied, "Not if we expect 'em to go on kissing us. I fear such misunderstandings just go with extended families. Likely just as well your surly cousin ain't wanted by the law."

Bob Ford scowled down at the herringbone bricks as he trudged on, muttering, "Yeah, lucky. What do you reckon might happen to a good old boy who turned in somebody he was sore at if that somebody had things he could pin on him in turn?"

Longarm said, "Might not be a good idea, long as the one he aimed to turn in was in a position to tattle on him. You know somebody in such a situation, Bob?"

Bob Ford blanched and said, "Perish the thought. Neither me nor my kid brother, Charley, have any truck with anybody wanted by the law and yonder's the Churchward place. It's been nice talking to you."

As the harmless-looking priss strode on, Longarm tethered the mule to the cast iron jockey by the curb and legged it up the steep walk to the steps of an imposing frame example of Steamboat Gothic carpentry.

A sort of butler uniformed like a U.S. Army sergeant major let him in and left Longarm to linger in the hall whilst he went to see if the general would receive a mere deputy.

The general would. He was more gracious than his stuck-up butler. The older man who received him in a sewing room fixed up like an office had snow white hair and a beard like Buffalo Bill Cody's. He never offered to shake but waved Longram to a seat across the desk from him and broke out a far nicer brand of cigar than Billy Vail smoked. He waited until they were lit up to ask Longarm what had brought him there.

Longarm said he'd heard about the general losing a white show horse.

The older man looked pained and reached in a desk drawer as he sighed, "Iceberg. Beautiful mount. Brought

152

him here from the Presidio of San Francisco when I retired last year. Stolen by a damned magician. Here's a photograph of the two of us together."

He handed a sepia tone print across the desk. Longarm only needed to take one glance at the image of a more imposing brigadier in full dress uniform aboard a friendly looking white horse with perked up ears to declare, "That's him. Your Iceberg is safe and sound, impounded just across the Big Muddy in Kansas at a town called Jubilee Junction, sir!"

"Thank God!" the older man sort of exploded, showing a relief he'd been holding in check, as an old soldier used to the shitty tricks Father Time and Lady Luck plays on all of us.

He wanted to know more. So Longarm brought him up to date on all he knew about the fortunately recovered Iceberg. Once he had the general he said, "That makes no sense! They went to so much trouble to steal him! Why would they abandon him like that, so soon?"

Longarm said, "When I figure that out, I may be able to say how come they stole those other horses of a different color. You say your Iceberg was stolen in a magical manner, General?"

General Churchward nodded and said, "Out of a veterinary clinic from behind a locked door, and get this, the door was still locked when they found Iceberg and another former Army mount missing in the morning!"

"They left horses locked in overnight with nobody on guard?" asked Longarm.

The older man said, "I wasn't there. But I understand there was a night watchman on duty, out front. He was supposed to look in on the patients in back from time to time. He says he did. Nobody knows when they were taken. He says they were there at four A.M. The other owner has brought suit against the veterinary, too. But that's neither here nor there. Why would anyone go to so much trouble if . . ."

"They might have been after the other mount, no offense," Longarm cut in, asking what Iceberg's owner could tell him about that.

The general couldn't tell him much. It seemed neither mount being kept overnight for observation had been really sick. Just off their feed and foaming at the mouth a mite. When Longarm asked if both mounts might have been branded on the near shoulder with that familiar U.S. the older man wasn't certain.

Longarm told him how to get in touch with the law in Jubilee Junction and in return got the local address of that veterinary.

It wasn't far and the veterinary was right pretty. The general had never told him Doc Sullivan was a she, going on thirty and trying to look older in her white smock with her brown hair pinned up in a severe bun. She seated Longarm in her office off the clinic, offered him no cigar and seemed mighty glad to hear at least one of her stolen patients had been recovered. She said the other horse they'd taken had been a standardbred about five years old. A two-hundred-dollar mount with no brand. Owned by a local banker who was sore as hell at her.

Longarm asked what had been wrong with the two critters left in her care. She said, "I couldn't say. That was why I was holding them for observation. I couldn't come up with anything with those symptoms that shouldn't have been effecting half the stock in Clay County. On the face of it I'd have said they'd both been fed laundry soap! But who on earth would do a thing like that?"

Longarm suggested, "Horse thief with keys to your clinic might. Let's think who'd be in position to feed soap to horses stabled apart from one another at the time. I got the impression, talking to him earlier, General Churchward didn't know the owner of that stolen bay. Can you come up with anywhere they might have tethered their mounts closer together?"

She said, "I can't, unless they frequent the same saloon or worse."

Longarm said he'd ask around. He didn't say where he meant to ask. A cathouse just made more sense than anywhere else. Pompous old men crave love and affection, too.

Figuring to be in town a spell, Longarm checked in to the modest hotel across from the Clay County Savings & Loan Association, the hometown bank Frank and Jesse had robbed right after getting home from the war. He left the mule in a nearby livery but locked his saddle and such in his hired room before he sauntered out to do some legwork. They called it legwork because it worked your legs and that was why he wore low heeled Army boots.

They had no whorehouses in their county seat, officiously. It was against the law to run a saloon in Dodge of late as well. Once he'd found their tenderloin district he treated himself to the noon supper he'd missed, consuming more grits and gravy, along with chicken-in-a-basket, along about three.

So it was midafternoon, a slow time for whores, when Longarm started at the top at Madame Celler Door's. After she'd weighed the likely outcomes of trying to bar entrance to a federal lawman or getting rid of him by telling him what she knew, Madame Celler Door told him the old fart on that snow white horse preferred the services of her rival, French Mabel. So he thanked her and headed on down cathouse row to interview the madam who offered more exotic and less tiring delights to dirty old men. It took a tad longer for her to come to much the same conclusions as Madame Celler Door. But once she had French Mabel confirmed that both General Churchward and Banker Applegate, though not known to one another, knew the same sucking wonders in the Biblical sense.

Longarm thus was able to confirm the two mounts stolen from the same veterinary clinic had been tethered side by side out front a lot.

Once he'd established that much the rest of the afternoon became a tedious familiar grind as Longarm blessed his stars and garters for those well-broken-in low-heeled boots. For it felt he covered all the streets of Liberty in them as he followed what Billy Vail called their process of elimination. He was bushed, thirsty and ready for more grub as his shadow lengthened on the walk ahead of him but he warned his appetites to wait on his duties and still just made it near closing time.

He found the fatherly locksmith alone in his cubbyhole shop near the center of things. As Longarm entered the locksmith told him they were fixing to close.

Longarm said, "No you ain't. You're fixing to open up and spill your guts to the only hope you have in this world, Mr. Bennet."

Locksmith Bennet blanched and said he was fixing to call the law.

Longarm said, "I am the law. Federal. So listen up. Being I'm federal means I don't *have* to run you in on a state offense. Are you with me so far?"

Bennet said he had no idea what he was talking about.

Longarm said, "Let me count the ways. You are a locksmith. You open locks for a living. They just let me read your yellow sheets over at the county prosecutors. You once did time for aiding and abetting. You let burglars into a pawnshop and you all got caught. You turned state's evidence and got off with six months. Took you five years to get your locksmith license back. If you get arrested on the same charge again you will never in this world get another license in this state or likely any other if Uncle Sam takes a personal interest in you. Do you want Uncle Sam to take a personal interest in you, Mr. Bennet?"

"I never took nothing. I was paid to open a door and I opened it. Is that a crime?"

Longarm said, "It sure was. Soaping those two expensive mounts so's they'd wind up behind that door you opened was mighty naughty as well. But, like I said, I'm federal and all I could charge you with would be tried in a state court."

He let that sink in before he added, "I'd as soon not waste needless time in a state court. But I can, and I will, unless you aim to save me some time here and now."

Before Bennet could bluster he snapped, "I ain't going to make that offer again. So what's it going to be?"

"What do you want to know?" asked the locksmith in a defeated voice.

So after he'd treated himself to a set down supper of steak and grits with fried collard greens, followed by peach pie and black coffee, Longarm paid another call on Doc Sullivan at her clinic.

She said *she* was fixing to close. So he walked her home as he told her what he'd found out, keeping his word to Bennet by not naming him.

He told her, "I hope to wrap the case up before anyone can sue you in court, Doc. I got it from a local informant . . . you were right about those valuable mounts being fed soft soap in hollowed carrots to make 'em foam at the mouth and feel awful. Once they were alone in the back of your clinic a sneak opened your back door with a skeleton key and the thieves led the poor critters out, not late at night, just after cock's crow, with the town starting to wake up as milk wagons rolled, other early deliveries commenced and nobody was likely to peer out a window when they heard other clip-clops. There were four of 'em. They walked the stolen mounts on out of town before they lit out for Kansas. The reason they got rid of the general's white Iceberg was they'd heard of trouble ahead. Seems the big boss mastermaster-minding the whole operation was having domestic troubles, with the wife who'd come up with horses of another color acting moody. They told the petty crook they were working with here another bunch had been led astray by the mastermind's woman. She'd given orders of her own that netted her some ready cash but left another member of the gang with egg on his face in the Arapaho County Jail."

She asked, "Arapaho County?"

He said, "Denver is in Arapaho County, Colorado. I told my boss he was sending me too far out in the field!"

The soberly handsome veterinary demured, "But his sending you this far led to your solving the case, right?"

To which Longarm could only reply, "Not hardly. It's opened a real can of worms on me."

She stopped in front of a garden gate to say, "This is my place. Why don't you come in and have some . . . coffee while you tell me more?"

Chapter 18

Cliches got to be cliches by being at least partway true. But Longarm had long since figured the reputation doctors, nurses and such had for sex mania might be inspired by their being pressed for free time and their having a more educated grasp on what was going on down there in their privates. Some of the meanest sex maniacs he'd ever arrested had been religious fanatics gone wrong.

Her name was Alice and it was a wonder how far she could let her hair down once she decided to let her hair down. She never unpinned it until he'd undressed the rest of her after they'd enjoyed some coffee and some wrestling on her sofa.

He undressed her in her bedroom. She said it was "shanty" to go all the way on a sofa. He didn't ask if she'd been getting any lately. From the way she wound up on top she'd been *wanting* some.

"That was lovely!" Doc decided as they took time out to slow their hearts back down before they burst. As he lit them a mutual smoke Doc asked what he'd meant by a can of worms.

He shook out the match, set it in the bedside ashtray and cuddled her fleshier charms against his naked flank before he replied, "Oh, that? I was talking about horse thieves that can't seem to make up their minds. This bigger federal case I was telling you about earlier would read more straightforward if some mastermind had come by some genuine but blank government forms and set up a fencing operation, selling off stolen stock as what seemed a safe bargain to many a buyer with a knowlege of horse teeth and a flexible conscience."

Doc Sullivan kissed his bare shoulder fondly and said, "I think you were ever so clever to have gotten as far as you have. With your investigation, I mean. What you've uncovered so far seems straightforward enough to me. Scattered smaller gangs across the county have been stealing Army horses before they were old enough to be sold off. Then subcontracting men such as that unfortunate Jefferson Boyd have been offering bargains only described as older standardbred with those forged Remount bills of sale appended to other phoney papers. What's so wormy about that, darling?"

He said, "Horses of another color. Jefferson Boyd might never have been caught in Denver if he hadn't had those outstanding Army grays on display half a day's ride from where look-alikes had been recently stolen."

She asked, "Didn't you get somebody to tell you some false-hearted woman had gotten him in that fix?"

He said, "I did. Seems a she-boss or the woman of the he-boss sold Boyd stock her husband had been holding in reserve. It was gray Army band stock stolen somewhere else."

"She must have hated him," the doc decided as another woman who likely knew about such feelings.

"She hated somebody," Longarm agreed. "But it might not have been old Jefferson. She might have been sore at someone else and just wanted Jefferson's ready cash. Only way she could have worked it called for her man, the real boss, being out of town at the time, leaving her in charge.

If the mastermind's headquarters are in Denver, I never should have left."

She purred, "I'm so glad you did. I might never have found out how they stole stock right out from under me! So chasing after horses of a different color hasn't been a total waste of time, has it?"

He let her have a drag on the cheroot as he replied, "Not total. Just distracting. Them band grays got Jefferson Boyd arrested and they had to murder him in jail before we could soften him up."

She asked, "What if he'd refused to talk? Did you really have enough on him to put him away, seeing he could produce papers in court to make it look as if he'd been duped by the real thieves?"

Longarm took the smoke back as he replied, "They couldn't chance his not making a deal to get out sooner. I figure this means he knew who the big boss was but had no closer ties than the so-called honor among thieves, which is as true a notion as fairies in the bottom of my garden. Boyd never let it show, but he must have been mad as a wet hen when he found out he'd been played false with them Army grays. The big boss must have been just as sore and twice as worried when he got back from whereever to discover what his woman had done."

He took a thoughtful drag and added, "We know how he handled the emergency at the jailhouse. Lord only knows where they hid the woman's body. But getting back to any colored horse but bay, the ones who wound up with General Churchward's white show horse got shed of it. And more recently a handsome black standardbred was used as a red herring to cover the theft of . . . Forget that. Wrong gang. But don't that prove the point of my puzzlement? Ain't no horse thief wants to steal stock that can be recognized from across the street."

She suggested, "Didn't you just answer that, darling? Didn't you say the thieves had gotten shed of most of those horses of another color without ever trying to sell them to anybody?"

He replied, "I did. So why did they steal them in the first place? Why have horses of another color you have to get rid of along the way when you could have left them where you found them? How tough would it have been to leave the general's Iceberg in his stall as they led that less distinctive bay out of his?"

She said, "I just thought of something. Crusader, the bay that was stolen, had never been in the Army. So he wore no Army brand or Army issue horseshoes. How could they have hoped to sell him off as surplus Remount stock?"

Longarm said, "Two ways. They could have unloaded him on another fence to be sold as was, some distance off with new provenance. Or, seeing they had a bunch of branded Army mounts with 'em when they had 'em reshod as civilians and left Iceberg with that colored blacksmith, they might brand unbranded standardbreds to pass for Army surplus."

She said, "That means at least one member of the gang might be a vet."

"Or an old cowhand," Longarm pointed out, adding, "Branding stock don't call for a college degree, you know."

She speculated, *"Neat* branding? A *lot* of neat branding? Keeping an eye out for excessive scarring or infection? Cattle spreads can afford to lose calves to infestation and they do. If your mastermind has branded expensive horseflesh he's working with a vet, if he's not a vet in his own right."

Longarm snuffed out the cheroot and wrapped both arms around her as he said, "You deserve a good kiss for that notion, Doc!"

She coyly asked, "Is that the best you can offer?"

So he cupped her firm chunky rump in both palms as he rewarded her more properly for suggesting a lead that could easily be checked out. He knew there were scores of veterinaries in the Arapaho County directory, but only some of them could have been out of town at the time those Army grays were stolen out to Camp Weld.

It wasn't until after they'd come it occurred to him all bets would be off if the mastermind had just hired a vet who never left town.

But what the hell, they'd both enjoyed the suggestion.

They tried some other suggestions before they finally caught some shut-eye and she served him marmalade on toast with tea for breakfast in bed. Doc said she'd been raised in the states and learned such old country notions from her Irish mother.

He said he was glad. Nobody made tea like Irish mothers and the varied breakfast menus a man with a tumbleweed job got to try made up for some of the mornings in the field he had to feed himself beans from the can.

Doc didn't want him to walk her back to her clinic. Like more than one impulsive young miss, she worried more about neighbors the morning after than the night before.

Longarm lay slugabed until nearly nine, treated himself to a shower thanks to her modern plumbing, and got dressed to stride boldly out the front door. He ticked his hat to the old woman fussing with fall mums in her own garden and said, "Morning, ma'am. I hate to be the one who has to tell you this, but them mums are dead. They might not know it yet, but that frost we had a couple of nights back means nothing we can do or say is ever going to get them to straighten up and bloom right."

She smiled uncertainly and asked, "Are you a gardener?"

He nodded and asked if she hadn't just seen him putting the doc's backyard to bed under mulch for winter.

Then he got out of there before she could ask or notice she ought to ask, where his tools might be.

He doubted she'd say anything to the doc about it later.

163

Nosey neighbors seldom wanted it known they were nosey and if she did, what the hell, it had been worth a try. Fifty-fifty was better than nothing.

He spent some time at the livery unloading that mule for less than he'd paid for it. The point was that you couldn't just run out on a gal or a mule and leave them stuck with the bill.

He considered that notion as he went on to his hotel to pick up his baggage. He still couldn't get it to work. Why steal a horse if you only meant to get shed of it later?

He had to change trains at Kansas City and that gave him some time to kill in the same. It was a pain in the ass when you had enough time between trains to wear out the sight-seeing around the station but not enough time to commence a flirtation or take in a show. As he passed a vaudeville theater handy to the station he saw he was fixing to miss out on a sure thing. The magical gal they had on the bill had waved his wand a lot for him that time up Montana way. But Billy Vail had never sent him out in the field to scout up old flames and even if Billy had, a lot of water had flowed under her britches and there was no saying such a warm-natured magician hadn't produced other rabbits out of her hat by now. So Longarm ambled on, feeling "Sophisticated" as he considered she would never know he'd just waved his wand at her some more from such a sensible distance in such a worldy way.

This English lady who'd taught him about such notions out in Frisco had explained "her kind" avoided the rolling on the floor brawling some less sophisticated folk indulged in by just not saying anything when they got caught or caught somebody rutting like a hog. Some of the "sophisticated arrangements" she'd described would have gotten many an old boy killed down on the farm.

That got him to wondering about that false-hearted woman who'd sold the late Jefferson Boyd a bill of goods in Denver. She might have been sore at her man for such doings or he might have been sore at her for the same. Long-arm was sure neither had let on to the neighbors, but as in the case of that fat Prince of Wales and Miss Lillie Langtry, a lot of the neighbors, and even more gang members, likely knew.

Then he was aboard his Denver-bound train, drumming on the sooty windowsill and humming that same tune in his head he'd been humming since he passed that theater back in K.C. He could just see himself traipsing all over Denver, asking strangers on the street, "Pardon me. Might you know a sophisticated veterinarian with a cheating wife or a mistress on the side who . . . son of a bitch! He must be a vet, or she's a vet or they're in tight as ticks with some vet!"

It was only when the dining car attendent came through, dinging those dinner chimes off-key from the tune in his head, that Longarm tumbled to what he'd been humming for hours.

It was a comical vaudeville song sung by the comical Eddie Foy with a comical lisp that time in Dodge. It told in mocking respect of a low-down dirty dog who cheated widows and orphans, stole pennies from blind news dealers or carried on worse than the Prince of Wales. Then it ended, "But he goes to church on Sunday! So they say he's an honest man!"

It sure beat all how bits and scraps of forgotten lore could creep out of the corners of your brain like so. Old Eddie Foy was suggesting they were looking for an up-standing pillar of the community who might be a doctor or more likely a vet with something going on in his *own* head about horses of a different color.

When he got into Denver after business hours he carried his awkward load home to his furnished digs and cleaned up after the long and sooty train ride. Someday somebody was going to make a fortune by inventing railroad locomotives that didn't belch soot and cinders, or mayhaps a way to take showers aboard a train. Longarm tended to come up with such inventions, if only he'd been able to get some backing. They went with paying attention to what was going on around him.

He stopped by that dry cleaners to find they'd had his tobacco tweed duty duds raring to go for some time. So he was properly dressed in the eyes of Miss Lemonade Lucy Hayes or Queen Victoria as he strode up the long slope of Capitol Hill and it was just as well. The fall evening was a tad crisp for denim.

The same nip in the air had made Billy Vail don a sheepskin jacket to smoke out on his steps. His wife had made him smoke out there. Longarm allowed she had a point. Billy's office down to the federal building reeked like a smokehouse.

Seated next to him with his own less pungent smoke, Longarm brought his boss up to date, concluding with, "Finding no further leads in the field and reconsidering that murder here in Denver, I figured it was time I got back to Denver."

Vail conceded, "That part makes sense. Run that bit about the mastermind being some sort of medical man by me again."

Longarm said, "I'm betting on a vet or a man with close ties to a vet. To begin with he knows more than most about the paperwork that goes with high-priced horseflesh. So would a vet. In the second place, as another vet assured me, there's more to branding an expensive mount than roping, throwing and holding him still with your boot and applying hot iron. After that, Jefferson Boyd was poisoned in his cell with strychnine. An animal poison. Not a sensible medication for humankind."

Vail said, "Oh, I don't know. I've heard some old-time sawbones prescribe strychnine in small doses for old age and most anyone can buy strychnine to rid themselves of wolves or coyotes at many a general store."

Longarm said, "Damn it, Boss, I never said it was a *sure* lead, I only said it was a *possible* lead!"

Vail let fly an awesome stinky cloud of smoke and decided, "I'll have Henry put some of the boys as ain't doing anything better on your notion. It's still mighty wild. But like you said, at least it's a possible and we sure as shit don't have anything better to work on!"

Longarm rose back to his considerable height and allowed he'd be on his way. Vail cocked a brow up at him to say, "I see the way you mean to go from here. You and that young widow woman ought to be ashamed of yourselves, carrying on like so and pretending nobody knows about the two of you!"

Longarm didn't answer. Old Billy had just given him something else to think about.

Chapter 19

"That was lovely, darling!" sighed the widow with the light brown hair as Longarm rolled off to let her breathe eaisier. Then she asked him why he was laughing like that.

When Longarm said he wasn't laughing at anything in particular she pouted, "I know what you were laughing at. It's my own fault for letting you do me dog style, earlier. I swear I've gained no more than five pounds in as many years but it all seems to settle in my poor old aunt Fanny Addams!"

He assured her he wouldn't want her to change a hair for him and that was the simple truth. Her still-shapely but softer curves had inspired him to new heights after the more chunky Doc, horsey Godiva, bubbly Simone and so forth. It was a caution how swell but different gals could turn out with their duds off. He'd almost forgotten this one's softer charms, sweet smile and quick mind. He could only hope she'd say something to piss him off before he wound up asking her to marry him.

He'd naturally brought her up to date on the confounding case he was still working on, down in her kitchen before she'd dismissed her cleaning char for the night and hauled him upstairs to take his beating like a man. So seeing there was time during a breather, Longarm said, "I'd like your opinion of sophistication, seeing you're a young sophisticated society gal who ought to know about such things."

"Have you been talking to Mrs. Vail about me again?" she demanded.

He said, "I never talk about you to anybody. Even when they ask me about you. And that ain't what I need to savvy better. Do you reckon Miss Augusta Tabor knows about her man, old Silver Dollar Tabor and that dim-witted blonde young enough to be their grandchild?"

She sniffed and said, "If she doesn't she's deaf, dumb and blind. A dirty old man who can resist showing off such a trophy is rare as a pool hall loafer admitting he's a virgin."

Longarm chuckled but asked, "Then how come old Hodd Tabor ain't been showing any visible bruises? Lord knows old Augusta is a lady in the original meaning of the word. They still go on about the way she nursed the sick and comforted the dying back when Leadville was still called Slabtown and they had no regular sawbones. But I understand she comes from humble stock."

The *rich* young widow with light brown hair told him, "You understand it all wrong. Hodd Tabor is the uneducated know-it-all who ran away from a Vermont farm and drifted aimlessly until he married a plain but well off and well-educated girl with a handsome dowry. Tabor used her money to chase the gold fever west and set up a general store. He'd have failed, talking big, if his more practical wife hadn't taken in washing, acted as local postmistress, opened bakeries and boardinghouses or . . ."

"Then Miss Augusta Tabor *is* a lady to the manor born and too worldly by nature to snatch Miss Elizabeth Baby Doe bald-headed! So I must be trying to cut the sign of a similar critter. A gal too worldly to kick up a fuss as she just bides her time to . . . do what? Get even or get away?"

The society gal snuggled up to him in the altogther warned him not to build castles in the air. She said, "Most women are far more sophisticated, and practical about such

170

matters than most men. We have to be. We start out growing up faster than boys. Then the boys grow up bigger and stronger and, thank God, more romantic."

"Ain't you gals supposed to be more romantic-natured?" he asked, even though he was inclined to follow her drift.

She laughed, with a hint of bitterness amid the good cheer, and told him, "The blushes and vapors are meant to soothe the savage beast. When a man has say sixty pounds and a longer reach on you, you'd be a fool to fight fair. Virgins are taught the blushes of the art while they still feel the blushes, and our hearts are trained to go pitty pat as required. Trust me. I know."

Then she remembered he wasn't one of the girls and reached down to take the matter in hand, assuring him, "Not that I'd ever try such stuff and nonsense on a man of the world, you understand!"

He understood. He never told her half what he was thinking, either. He said, "Leaving aside the background of a false-hearted woman, would a woman really sore at a horse thief want to cover up for him? Mayhaps for old time's sake?"

She thought and decided, "It's hard for a woman who's given herself to a man not to feel something for him. Some say Delilah wept for Samson after she'd done him dirt. On the other hand, would you want the law to catch a horse thief if you were still married to him?"

Longarm held her closer as he marveled, "I don't know, it hardly seems fair to pack so many brains and such a fine ring-dang-doo in one bodacious wrapping of delicious she-male flesh!"

"What did I say? Not that I'm complaining!" she laughed as he slid his free hand down her soft torso to part some soft brown hair.

There were times for talking and times for action, so, seeing she'd said all that needed saying, he acted like a man showing a pal how much he appreciated her help.

Later seeing as, being a woman, she wasn't willing to just count her blessings and enjoy 'em, he explained, "You explained away a jammed log that was key to the whole log jam. Now that facts and figures are flowing free to be added up sensible I only need to make sure of a few facts to flush the birds from cover and make some sensible arrests!"

She asked who the mastermind was.

He said, "Can't say, yet. But I suspect I know how to find out. So why don't we wear ourselves to a frazzle and see if we can catch us some sleep? I fear I face a busy day, come morning!"

He hadn't said the half of it as other facts and figures got to coming in from all over in answer to questions Longarm had not been alone in asking. Henry had already received a list of code numbers from the Government Printing Office, cornfirming those Remount Service blanks had been sent to Fort Leavenworth, albeit never received, and replace by yet another batch. Henry had suggested they put out a warrant for whoever opened Remount's mail at Fort Leavenworth. Longarm shook his head and said, "That ain't the way the Army does things, Henry. Anybody accepting mail from off post has to sign for it if he's the one it's addressed to. But before it gets to him it's handed around some. So why don't we wire Fort Leavenworth and find out if any recent deserters were assigned to mail sorting before they lit out?"

Henry said he'd get on it. It was Reporter Crawford of the *Denver Post* who told them about that veterinary convention in Chicago around the time Camp Weld was visited by horse thieves. The stout derby-hatted cuss with a nose for news said he could save them some time by wiring a pal on the *Chigago Tribune*.

Crawford said, "You don't need or want a list of everyone who attended. Just the names of vets from *Denver,* right?"

Longarm told him that was about the size of it, adding, "Already noticed how many such gents we have in our

172

county directory. Take me a month of Sundays to check 'em all out and I only want the names of our likely suspects."

He had less luck, himself, at that fancy women's shop on 17th Street. Even wearing a suit and tie and flashing his badge and I.D. the imperious dowager in charge, who looked as if she'd hated boys since one of 'em put her braid in an inkwell, insisted such information was what she called privileged.

It likely was. So he went up to the brownstone Tabor mansion atop Capital Hill and asked to speak with another dowager.

Longarm and Miss Augusta Tabor went back to the time he'd foiled a brazen burglary attempt up yonder whilst she'd been up in Leadville. Rich folk lived all over. A butler who looked too stuck up to serve anyone below the rank of Queen Victoria showed him into the front parlor where the plain but pleasant Miss Augusta heard him out over tea and scones. As soon as she followed his drift she had her maids gussie her up whilst her coachman brought her berlin and four around to the front.

Then the two of them drove down to the flats and made a grand entrance at that grand shop. Miss Augusta didn't ask the dowager in charge for a private conversation in the back. She announced they were fixing to have one.

Longarm still expected to witness some arm twisting. But when the formidable Augusta said she wanted the home address of a Penelope Mansfield she'd sold a silk lined carpetbag to the old gal told her right off that the best she could do might be a Pamela *Westfield*.

Augusta Tabor glanced at Longarm, who said, "Close enough," and they left with Pamela Westfield's home address in his notebook.

As he explained to the pal who'd helped him, seeing her off from the corner of Colfax and Broadway, he had to hold the thought until he gathered more evidence. She dimpled down at him from her berlin as she made him promise she'd hear the end of the story from him before it ever appeared in the papers, adding, "See that you keep Hodd and me out of those damned papers for a change!"

He followed her drift. It was doubtless a pain to read about your husband and a bubblehead too young for your son to mess with.

They said the full grown Nat Tabor had fussed with his father in vain about Baby Doe. But it seemed there was no fool like an old fool with a hard-on. For having seen the both of them in the flesh, if only with their clothes on, Longarm would have gone to bed with old Augusta first. He'd never felt sorely tempted to screw dumb animals.

He was tempted to jump the gun as ever more evidence came in. But he wanted to present the case to the fair but firm Judge Dickerson down the hall with the box nailed shut on the sneaky son of a bitch.

So he waited until wires from all over confirmed the way he'd put the picture together at last. Then he hired a hack so's nobody would have to walk to the Federal House of Detention downtown and told the coachman to just set tight as he paid a call at a veterinary clinic run by a Doctor Wilberforce Westfield, or so it said.

A pallid assistant who sort of reminded Longarm of Henry at the office led him back to where the doc was just taking a hypodermic needle out of a mangy-looking old basset hound on a zinc-topped table.

Westfield told Longarm with a sad smile, "Had to put old Shep, here, down. As I told his owners, there's only so much one can do for a dog this old."

Old Shep looked up at Longarm and wearily wagged his tail. Westfield was a man about Longarm's age, a tad shorter and built thicker. Albeit that looked like muscle under his white lab coat.

Longarm asked, "Are you sure you gave him enough, Doc?"

Westfield sounded smug as he replied, "I always do. I guess I ought to know what I am doing."

Longarm nodded and said, "I guess you must. They tell me Jefferson Boyd, over to the jailhouse, was poisoned by somebody who knew just what he was doing. Neither too little nor too much."

Westfield stepped clear of the dog on the table with the hypodermic in hand, letting his eyes flick down to Longarm's gun grips for less time than most might have noticed as he asked in an innocent tone who Jefferson Boyd might have been.

Longarm said, "You both had me going with horses of a different color. Had I stayed on the damned tracks I'd have been by here sooner. If it's any comfort to you, Doc, she kept trying to protect you even as she was running away from you. You should have heard how earnest she sounded as she went on about those horses of a different color meaning more than they really did."

"She? Who are you talking about? *What* are you talking about!" the cuss he had the goods on tried.

Longarm said, "Aw, come on, her real name was Pamela, as you know, but she introduced herself to me as Penny when she tried to sort of join me to help in the investigation. You should have let her. She really had me barking up wrong trees until you almost caught us in the act in K.C. and she had to light out on both of us."

Westfield conceded, "I do have a wife named Pamela, or I did until she left me some time ago."

Longarm said, "Wasn't all that long ago. She lit out on you when she had the chance, with you at that convention in Chicago. Don't say you never 'tended it. We got you there on paper."

Westfield said, "I was in Chicago recently. What of it?"

Longarm said, "She was afraid of you. Considering the way you trailed after her far as K.C. she might have had just cause. Possessive gents like you don't let a woman have much mad money at her disposal. You let her charge anything from groceries to silk-lined carpetbags all over town. But she needed mad money to get home and when you were off to that convention in Chicago, leaving her in nominal charge as the lady of the house, she saw her chance. You had those six grays stolen elsewhere held in reserve. You sold 'em to Jefferson Boyd, who hadn't heard about grays stolen recently from Camp Weld. The rest we know. Having shortstopped your usual cut she packed one carpetbag and lit out. I don't know, yet, whether she planned on joining the investigation from the start or just proved once more she thought fast on her feet. I'll ask her when we extradite her from Georgia and . . . No! Don't try it!"

But the desperate Westfield must have known he had no other choice but to try and had Longarm not sucked in his gut as he crawfished he'd have taken that needle still half filled with poison where it would have done him no good at all. Westfield had aimed for his aorta.

Then the desperate killer's world blew up in his face and he was flat on his back with his world spinning round as he stared up through swirling gunsmoke at the lawman standing over him.

Longarm told him, not unkindly, "I told you not to try, Doc."

Westfield groaned, "You *shot* me, you son of a bitch! But *how*?"

Longarm held his double derringer up to the light as he replied in a friendlier tone, "Saw how you kept glancing down at my pistol grips. We could both see I'd never crossdraw faster than you could strike with that needle in your hand. But, knowing in advance I was dealing with a devious cuss, I had this devious derringer palmed on you all the time."

The pale youth who'd shown him back there tore in with

a worried expression to ask, "What happened? I heard what sounded like a gunshot and . . . oh dear Lord!"

Longarm said, "I told you out front I was the law. Now I'd like you to tell my coachman to fetch us some more law, here."

He glanced down at Westfied and added, "Tell him we need somebody from the coroner's office, too."

Chapter 20

A bee swarm without a queen bee could still sting and a confederacy of horse thieves deprived of its brains could have still caused heaps of trouble for all concerned. But with the murderous Westfield's devious misdirecting out of the way, mopping up the mess he'd left went a lot smoother.

By the time the coroner's jury had officiously found the cause of Westfield's death to be serious internal bleeding, occasioned by one derringer round nicking his heart, his misdirecting wife was back from Georgia, sincerely needing the shower they treated her to at the women's wing of the Federal House of Detention.

Billy Vail informed Longarm of the same and asked how they'd done it when his senior deputy reported in the next morning.

Settling down and lighting up, Longarm said, "We couldn't have done it without the help of Western Union and Henry's opposite number at the Cobb County Clerk's Office near Atlanta, where they picked her up for us. But I'm getting ahead of my story."

Settling back as best one could in an uncomfortable guest chair on his side of Vail's cluttered desk, Longarm explained, "Doc Westfield had put together a smooth fencing operation with a slick marketing strategy but he knew more about handling horses than women. He must have thought they needed as firm a hand on their reins. The spoiled southern belle he held on a short lead saw her chance to make a break for it when he went off to that Chicago convention. She'll know better than us whether he was chump enough to leave her in charge out our way or whether she misdirected the boys to believe he had. She was a wonder at misdirecting boys. In any case she sold stock they had on hand to the one and original Jefferson Boyd, who didn't know we were looking for matching stock recently stolen out to Camp Weld. Then she packed a carpetbag with newspaper, padded away from the premises and hopped a train for home with her real baggage the mad money in her smaller purse. You'll have to ask her if she knew all along who I was or only figured it out after I told her. Either way, she didn't want us catching her husband before she was in the clear with room to spare, even though she was sore at him. So she misdirected me, or at least she tried to, by suggesting those horses of a different color would lead me to the promised land."

Vail nodded and said, "I got that part clear enough. They were using them distinctive mounts as razzle dazzle whilst they unloaded Army bays they didn't want us thinking about. How come you just said *I* should ask? Don't you work here anymore?"

Longarm didn't answer. As he searched for a delicate way to put it the older lawman cocked a brow to ask, "Did you go and compromise your old organ grinder in a *suspect*, you randy young cuss?"

Longarm sheepishly replied, "I didn't know she was a suspect, yet. I told you she was smooth and it was a long trip. By the time I had call to even suspect she was running away from another man she'd had her way with my weak nature. I only managed to put it together after the milk had been spilled all over everybody. I figure once Wesfield got back from Chicago to find his woman gone and Jefferson Boyd sore as hell about that and under lock and key, Westfield began by murdering Boyd to keep him quiet and cover that base. Then, knowing where his runaway wife was likely to run, he hopped a train to chase her, but found he'd hopped too early a train and things went like one of them French bedroom farces until he got warm in K.C."

Vail said, "Had he caught you aboard that steamboat with her, before you'd even guessed she was a runaway wife . . ."

Longarm grimaced and said, "It was close enough as it turned out. His wife spotted him first and gave him the slip. He stayed aboard or found out later the handsome galoot his bad Penny had been keeping company with had gone on up to Fort Leavenworth. He didn't know I was a lawman on his trail when he paid those local guns to do me. He thought he was setting up his wife's lover. He must have shit when he found out, later, who I was, and that Penny-Pamela wasn't with me. So he beelined back to Denver and hoped in vain for the best. The rest you know."

Vail objected, "No I don't. How did you figure out who he was, or where his wife had gone?"

Longarm explained, "The one led to the other. I noticed how a woman being paged as a Wesfield had told me she was a Mansfield. I figured the first name would be close as well. You were the one who told me way back when how even suspects who change their names entire like to hang on to fond memories. By any name our bad Penny wanted it known she was a southern belle of quality and, seeing her old plantation had been burnt out by Sherman's bummers she felt no call to change such golden childhood memories."

Taking a drag and flicking some ash for the carpet mites, Longarm went on, "Hoping she might have been talking about real times and places I wired the Cobb County Clerk, near Kenneswa Mountain, and damned if there hadn't been a Twelvetrees Plantation in that neck of the woods."

Vail nodded and said, "After that all we needed was the record of any daughter of the house marrying up with . . . ?"

"He had her paged under her married name," Longarm explained, adding, "After that I only had to get their home address here in Denver from the shop where a Mrs. Westfield had bought a mighty fancy carpetbag. Can I go out and play, now?"

Vail laughed and said, "Not hardly. You got courtroom duty down the hall, seeing I have to pay your call on Pamela Westfield."

So Longarm did as Billy Vail pointed the facts of nature out to the wide-eyed innocence of Pamela Westfield née Culpepper of Twelvetrees.

Once she'd been made to see how much time off the fair but firm Judge Dickerson was likely to grant her for turning states evidence Longarm got the chore of rounding up the bunch who'd really stolen horses out to Camp Weld.

Penny-Pamela hadn't been taken in to her late husband's full confidences, but she suspected the real Army gray, held out at a homestead to the southeast, would have been turned loose on the prairie in time to confuse hell out of everyone. She couldn't say why Westfield had brought in the gray she'd sold Jefferson Boyd. She hadn't really cared.

Billy Vail gave Longarm the lethal team of fellow deputies known as Smiley and Dutch to back his play.

Deputy Smiley was a tall dark hatchet-faced breed who'd never smiled in human memory. Smiley had been the family name on the white side.

Nobody could pronounce the family name of the deputy they just called Dutch. Dutch was shorter, fairer and smiled a lot, even as he beat you to the draw.

Together they were almost as dangerous to mess with as Longarm, with the cooler Smiley holding the deadly Dutchman in check, whilst Dutch had saved Smiley's bacon on occasion by drawing impossibly fast at the last possible moment.

On their way to a seedy hotel near the stockyards Longarm told the two of them, "We're after a professional horse thief posing as a cattle buyer when he ain't serving as a noncom with the Colorado State Guard. This offers him easy access to Army blues and he knows his way around a military reserve serving state and regular troops. We figure they led bays to be sold and grays to misdirect off post in broad-ass daylight, using a version of the old cardboard folder trick."

"Cardboard what?" asked Dutch.

The saturine Smiley said, "Army recruits learn the first day that if some officers spy a chocolate soldier standing still he's sure to ask him why. So you carry a cardboard folder under one arm and keep moving, with a serious expression. Otherwise they are surely going to put you to work at something harder."

Longarm allowed that was about the size of it and added, "Nobody is likely to question a uniformed work detail as it herds Remount stock most anywhere."

They got to the hotel. Longarm sent Smiley and Dutch to cover the back stairs as he went up the front with a drawn six-gun in one hand and a passkey from the scared-looking desk clerk in the other.

On the top floor he found the hired door of the part-time guardsman wide open. The cigar he'd been smoking had left a sort of locomotive smoke trail out the door and toward the back. As Longarm chased after him he heard a fusilade of gunshots, followed the bumping and thumping of somebody headed downstairs the uncomfortable way.

"Smiley? Dutch?" Longarm called from the head of the stairs.

"I told the fool to freeze," called Dutch in a cheerful tone.

Rounding up that ones known associates in Denver took almost a week.

By then one of the bounty jumpers who'd worked in the mail room over at Fort Leavenworth had been picked up trying to pull the same stunt at Fort Sill by a sharp-eyed recruiting sergeant.

Faced with the choice of "Death or such other punishment as the court-martial shall decide," he'd chosen to talk.

So crooks commenced to fall like apples from the tree, now that the law was shaking the tree instead of chasing after horses of another color.

That formidable dowager at the fancy shop helped them get more out of Penny-Pamela than she might have meant to give them, once she chose to press charges for shoplifting.

When Vail explained to the runaway bride that charging a handsome new carpetbag to your husband's account, after it could be proven by witnesses you'd left his bed and board, constituted grand theft in the eyes of Colorado Statute Law. So damned if old Penny-Pamela didn't manage to tie up more loose ends for everybody.

Some few lesser lights slipped through the cracks, of course—they always did—free to mend their ways or get caught the next time.

Longarm granted an interview to the helpful Reporter Crawford but asked if the *Post* could hold the story a spell, explaining he'd promised another pal she'd get it from him instead of the papers.

When Crawford allowed his paper wouldn't run the story before it came off the presses in the morning, Longarm said that was good enough. So they shook and parted friendly.

The same snooty butler let Longarm in but sounded almost human as he led the way to the front parlor of the Tabor mansion, warning Longarm to, "Be gentle with the madam, sir. She's had a trying day."

Longarm doffed his hat as he joined the lady of the house in gloom. None of the new Edison bulbs had been switched on. Such illumination as there was came through lace curtains from the streetlamp out front.

So the plain but ladylike Augusta was a sort of forlorn outline as he joined her, hat in hand.

She said it was good of him to come.

He said, "I told you I might, Miss Augusta. Soon as we wrapped up that case you helped us with."

She replied, "Oh, that? I thought you'd read about us in the papers. You're one of the few friends I can count on not to snicker."

She sobbed and sort of whispered, "Oh, Custis, you're one of the few friends I have *left*!"

He sat down beside her, got rid of his hat, and took one of her hands in both of his to say, "That ain't so, Miss Augusta. You got lots of friends from here to all along the Front Range. You're famous, Miss Augusta. And in all of the times I've heard your name mentioned from mining camps to social gatherings up here on the hill, I have never heard one word said against you!"

She sighed and replied, "You must have wax in your ears, then. Or dosen't it count when people dismiss a discarded old baggage with wry pity?"

He insisted, "Ain't heard nobody chuckle at you, Miss Augusta. What in thunder is this all about?"

She hauled his hands cupped around hers into her lap as she told him, "Hodd's asked me for a divorce! He means to cast me aside after all these years and marry that . . . child."

Longarm didn't answer. He didn't know what he might say. He noticed even as she revealed the scandal she never mean-mouthed Baby Doe. So he held his tongue as to what he thought of a man who'd leave a woman for a retarded pretty child.

She told him, "Hodd says he means to do right by me. He says he knows what he owes to me. Wants us to go on being friends. Have you ever heard of such a situation, Custis?"

Longarm said, "Yep. They say Princess Alexandra of

Wales invited her husband's mistress, Miss Lillie Langtry, to tea, seeing they had so much in common."

The Colorado mining queen laughed despite herself and gasped, "Good heavens, did Miss Langtry come?"

Longarm said, "Not hardly. So the princess scored one up on her in the game of acting worldly. Bad manners betray a lack of sophistication and it's bad manners to turn down an invite to tea from a princess."

Augusta Tabor laughed again and said, "By the Great Horned Spoon I'm tempted! What do you think Baby Doe would do or say if I told the two of them they had my blessings and thought we should all get together with our friends for a swell bash?"

She suddenly swept him into her arms and kissed him. She kissed pretty good, too. Then she shoved him away and said, "Silly me. You always seem to cheer me up, Custis Long. I swear if I went in for that sort of revenge . . . But never mind, I don't, and I think you had better be on your way now!"

So he went his way, crunching fallen leaves, with his lips still undecided as they tingled. For damned if that hadn't felt like kissing a young gal!

As he walked he wondered if he might be going *loco en la cabeza*. For the likeable old Augusta had never been a beauty to begin with and now she was old enough to be his mother, but . . .

"Wouldn't that be something to marvel about?" he laughed to himself and dismissed the odd notion, at least for the time being.

But later that night, when a way younger and far prettier society gal asked him what he was laughing at as he plumbed her depths, Longarm could only reply, "Nothing. Nothing at all possible."

For he knew she'd neither understand nor approve the picture that had just popped into his fool head, involving her, old Augusta and the battle-axe from that fancy shop downtown.

Watch for

LONGARM AND THE
BAD BREAK

the 326th novel in the exciting LONGARM
series from Jove

Coming in January!

**Explore the exciting Old West with one
of the men who made it wild!**